ELIZABETH OLDFIELD

Looking After Dad

Harlequin Books

TORONTO • NEW YORK • LONDON
AMSTERDAM • PARIS • SYDNEY • HAMBURG
STOCKHOLM • ATHENS • TOKYO • MILAN
MADRID • WARSAW • BUDAPEST • AUCKLAND

ISBN 0-373-11879-1

LOOKING AFTER DAD

First North American Publication 1997.

Copyright © 1997 by Elizabeth Oldfield.

This edition published by arrangement with Harlequin Books S.A.

Printed in U.S.A.

CHAPTER ONE

IT WAS one of those days when it would have been smarter to ignore the bossy beep-beep of the alarm, pull the covers up high over her head and stay in bed.

Clutching a half-eaten prawn and mayonnaise sandwich in one hand and with a magnum of champagne in the other, Jess Pallister sped along the busy city street. First she had forgotten to buy fresh muesli so had had to miss breakfast, then the showers at the pool were out of order, next she had received a worrying gift, and finally, when she was looking forward to a calm afternoon at her easel, an unexpected interview had been sprung on her.

She was a darn sight too pliable, Jess thought as she swerved to avoid a youth dispensing a confetti of 'cheap pizza' vouchers. Instead of saying an outright, blunt and forestalling *no*, she had listened—and allowed herself to be sweet-talked into going along.

'Sounds like a dream assignment,' her brother had declared, when relaying the brief details, but she had been on what he had claimed were 'dream' assignments before and they had turned out to be nightmares. Her fingers tightened around the throat of the champagne bottle. Like the one with Roscoe Dunbar.

Reaching a glistening white tower block, Jess pushed around revolving doors and into a vast marble-floored lobby. A look was snatched at her watch. She hated to be late and there was five minutes to spare. Five minutes in which to finish her lunch on the hoof and present herself—cool, calm and collected—at the twentieth and top-floor offices of Sir Peter Warwick, business tycoon and international hotelier.

She scanned the bank of lifts and on seeing one with doors smoothly closing leapt forward. Using her bulging sports bag as an impromptu battering ram, she hurtled in through the gap, which forced the half-dozen or so occupants into a collective backwards shuffle.

'Made it,' she mumbled, shining a general smile of apology, and turned to inspect the wall indicator panel. Someone had already pressed the '20' lozenge.

As the lift began to rise, Jess took another bite of her sandwich. She might have been persuaded to attend the interview, but that did not mean she would be pliable again and meekly accept the job. No chance. As Kevin had acknowledged it was her decision, and it only required one snag and she intended to refuse. Mutiny simmered in her hazel brown eyes. The days of being Miss Amenable were over. From now on, she did what she wanted to do and ran her life *her* way.

The lift stopped to allow a couple of middle-aged men with briefcases to get out and, in the pause, Jess ate the remainder of her sandwich. As the ascent re-started, she licked crumbs from the corners of her mouth and wiped her fingers on a tissue. Before she faced the business tycoon lipstick needed to be applied and her hair brushed through, but she would do that when the surprisingly lethargic lift reached the top floor.

Jess hitched the sports bag higher onto her shoulder. Her fellow passengers were all prime examples of city-smart sartorial elegance, whereas in a paint-dotted pastel pink tunic and black leggings which looked as if they might date from the Battle of Trafalgar she was casual. Casual, flustered and disgruntled. Lowering her head, she gave a discreet sniff. Yuck. She also smelled faintly of chlorine.

For a second time the lift halted, disgorged people and resumed its leisurely journey. Now the only other occupant was a man who stood beside the opposite wall. She cast him a glance. With his arms folded across his chest and his head bent, he was lost in thought. He looked sombre and tense. As if this September day had not turned out to be exactly a bundle of laughs for him, either.

He was in his late thirties, tall—she estimated around six feet four—and had a lean, rangy frame. Thick dark hair fell over his forehead in engaging windswept disarray and his skin bore the golden remains of a tan. Clad in an immaculate navy pinstriped suit, he looked like a business executive; yet the hair, which was worn long enough to brush his collar, and a jazzy pink, blue and white patterned silk tie suggested he was not the conventional city type, but had a touch of the maverick about him.

She could not see his eyes, but he had a broad brow, straight nose and granite jaw. His features were too tight-drawn for him to be classified as handsome, yet even standing still he possessed an inherent masculine *vibrancy* which made him magnetic. The darkness, almost blue-black, of his hair hinted at a Latin lineage . . . or could it be Irish? She settled on Irish. His mood seemed tinged with the melancholy of the Celt.

He would be someone who was accustomed to command, she assessed, and who did not suffer fools—

Abruptly realising that the man had noticed her examination and was looking coolly and somewhat aggressively back, Jess switched her gaze to the indicator panel. Did he think she had been sizing him up? As other women had doubtless sized him up on numerous occasions before. If so, he was wrong. Her job meant she was trained to be observant and to take note, and he had intrigued her as a case study, that was all. She chewed at her lip. Should she make a comment—perhaps about his tie—which would show she had absolutely no personal interest and defuse the situation?

As the light illuminated for the eighth floor, she turned towards him. 'I do like—'

Bang! The champagne exploded. The cork shot out from the bottle like the obligatory speeding bullet, whistled past the man's ear and thudded with a thwack against the wall behind him. Ribbons of white foam followed, spurting crazily. All of a sudden, it was New Year's Eve.

Startled, Jess jumped. She blinked. Her mouth fell open and she gaped. The man was being sprayed. He had brought his right arm up to shield his eyes, but froth was spewing over his dark hair, across the width of his broad shoulders, splattering like fast-melting snow on the pinstriped jacket.

'Oh, dear!' she bleated, holding helplessly onto the magnum with two hands as the foam turned into a high-pressure liquid jet.

Now champagne rained onto his face, swamped his sleeve, was flowing in fast bubbly rivulets down his suit.

'Away,' the man rasped.

Jess looked blankly at him through the downpour. 'I beg your pardon?'

'Hold the bloody bottle away!' he bellowed.

'Oh . . . yes.'

She straightened up the magnum, which meant the champagne hit the roof of the lift like a geyser and showered down onto the two of them. Though only for a moment for, with a violent oath, the man leapt forward, grabbed hold of the neck and directed the torrent down and into a corner. There it gushed for a couple more seconds before diminishing into a harmless dribble.

'For God's sake!' he rasped, glaring at her.

His eyes proved to be an astonishing pale blue, fringed with thick black lashes. They were beautiful eyes, the kind of eyes about which poets waxed lyrical and whose soft gaze would reduce maidenly hearts to marshmallow—though right now they blazed with the hard flame of anger.

'I'm very sorry,' Jess said. 'Everything happened so fast, I was taken by surprise.'

'But why did it happen?' her victim demanded, swiping hanks of dripping jet-black hair back from his brow.

'I've no idea,' she replied, and stopped.

A giggle had bubbled up in her throat. He looked so furious and bedraggled that, all of a sudden, his plight took on a comical air and she was stricken by an acute urge to laugh. Or was it nerves? Whatever, if the last couple of minutes had been videoed and shown on prime-time 'Candid Camera' TV, audiences worldwide would be in tucks.

'Don't risk it,' he warned, showing himself to be disconcertingly alert.

Jess gulped down the giggle. He was in no mood to join her in mutual mirth. Indeed, if her lips as much as twitched she would be inviting mayhem.

'The bottle was secure when I took it out of the box half an hour ago,' she continued, now resolutely straight-faced, 'and all I've done is come here.'

Pulling a white handkerchief out of his pocket, the man began to mop his face and hair. 'You ran?' he asked, and answered his own question. 'Yes, when you barged into the lift and damn near knocked everyone flying, you were bright red and panting.'

Jess's lips tightened. He exaggerated. There had been no danger of her knocking into anyone. Nor did she appreciate his 'bright red' comment, which made her sound like a beetroot. To be wearing grungy clothes was disadvantage enough without him downgrading her appearance.

'I have an appointment and am short of time,' she said, in a taut justification.

'So you jogged and bounced up the champagne?' His lip curled. 'Great!'

The lift was slowing for the sixteenth floor. When the doors opened should she make a quick exit? Jess wondered. Escape might be the coward's way out, yet it was tempting in that it would save her from more embarrassment and the risk of further condemnation. But, though the lift had dallied on the point of stopping, it suddenly speeded up again. Floor sixteen had come and gone.

With a disgusted look at his now sodden handkerchief, the man pushed it gingerly back into his pocket. 'Pity the cork didn't pop when the lift was full, then you could've drenched *en masse* and really had a chuckle,' he said, in a low, gravelly voice which, she registered, contained a trace of an American accent.

'I didn't do it on purpóse,' Jess protested.

'You just didn't think?'

She glowered. Must he be so accusing and patronising—and so right?

'No,' she was forced to agree.

Again the lift reduced speed, dawdled tantalisingly around the seventeenth floor and went at full lick again.

'Do you suppose we might break down?' she asked, in sudden alarm.

Enduring his company now was bad enough, but to be trapped with him—maybe for hours!—would be a real bed of nails.

'It wouldn't surprise me. Nothing would surprise me,' the man said, as though she might have been tinkering with the lift's motor and was responsible for its malfunction. 'But if we're marooned I shan't be a happy bunny, especially as I also have an appointment and—' looking down at his suit, he spread his hands in a curt gesture of impatience '—I'm wet through.'

'I'm sorry,' Jess said again.

'I should damn well think you are!'

She bridled. She resented being bawled out quite so thoroughly.

'Tell me, are you always this tetchy?' she enquired.

'When I'm doused in champagne from head to foot, pretty much.'

'It was an accident,' she defended.

He arched a brow. 'The hand of fate?'

'*Yes.*' Putting down the bottle, Jess rooted around in her sports bag and found a tissue. 'Let me soak up the worst.'

In grim silence, her victim held out his arm and she began to blot at his sleeve. All of a sudden, she halted. The tissue she was using was the one she had used to wipe her fingers and now a streak of pale lemon mayonnaise smeared the fine navy cloth.

The man raised his eyes as if appealing to the heavens to grant him forbearance. 'Why don't I strip off all my clothes and you can jump up and down on top of them,' he suggested, 'and perhaps kick them around the floor for a while?'

Jess gave a strained smile. She wanted to kick herself—and him. 'It won't stain,' she vowed, finding a wad of new tissues and frantically scrubbing, and to her huge relief the mayonnaise disappeared.

As he stood erect and cautious, she mopped the wet from his shoulders and started to dab at his chest. Her pulse rate quickened. She might be performing a practical chore for a hostile stranger, yet it was difficult to ignore the muscled physique beneath his clothes. It was also difficult not to imagine what he would look like if he *did* strip naked. Lithe, honey-skinned and of Greek god proportions.

'No more,' the man instructed, taking a sudden step backwards.

Jess looked at him. He wanted her to stop, but why? Surely he had not recognised her rising tension and—oh, horror—sensed her vivid imaginings?

Don't be silly, she told herself, he's not a mind reader. It must be a case of him being affected by the physical contact, too. Even if her face had been red and might still be a little pink, she was not too hard on the eye. Indeed, her combination of blonde gamine looks, tall, slim figure and long legs had been known to make men go weak at the knees.

Jess was smugly congratulating herself on having unsettled *him*, when she realised that the damp tissues had begun to break up and were leaving tiny white flecks over his jacket. She groaned. Why, when he had confirmed her assessment of him as not suffering fools, must she play the clown with her every move?

'I should never've got up this morning,' she muttered.

'It would have made my life one heck of a sight easier,' the man agreed stingingly.

'The bits'll come off,' she said, refolding the tissues to a dry patch.

He raised a long-fingered hand. 'Leave it,' he ordered.

'But—'

'Would you do me a favour and keep away from me? Well away.'

She stuffed the tissues back into the sports bag. So much for trying to help—and so much for her sex appeal. The only way to make his knees weaken would be to hit them with a mallet!

The lift was stopping and when Jess looked at the panel the light showed that, in her do-gooder confusion, the slow-pause-start procedure at the two previous floors had passed unnoticed and they had reached their destination. Heaven be praised.

'I'll pay for your suit to be cleaned,' she said, delving in amongst her swimming gear to find her purse.

'Thanks for the offer, but there's no need.'

'I'd like to pay.'

The man hoisted a brow. 'With what—notes which glue themselves to the hand or dye the skin bright purple or give off that fragrant aroma of swimming pool which I've detected? If you don't mind, I'll pass.'

Her temper flared. The yellow flecks burned in her hazel eyes. Where pure unvarnished sarcasm was concerned, he ranked as a Grand Master.

'I do mind,' she began to insist, but he ignored her.

'I've enjoyed spending time with you. I wouldn't have missed it for the world. Indeed, my only regret is that we shall never meet again,' he said, his tone as dry as dust, and as the doors slid aside he stepped out onto the wide pale-carpeted corridor and strode away.

Jess stuck out her tongue at his broad back. It might have been a juvenile yah-boo response, yet it felt immensely satisfying.

She frowned down at the note which she held in her hand. Her instinct was to chase after him and thrust it stubbornly into his pocket—why should he be allowed to dictate everything?—but after a moment she returned it to her purse. She had no wish to be ordered to keep away again and, in any case, once she embarked on a full-time painting career she was going to need all available cash.

Her eyes went to the champagne-spattered walls and patch of soggy carpet. The lift required attention. Walking out to drop the empty bottle into a convenient waste bin, she looked up and down the corridor. The stranger had disappeared off to the right, but in the distance on the left two women in overalls were chatting beside a vacuum cleaner. She alerted them to the state of the lift and asked for directions to the ladies' room.

Jess washed her hands, coloured her lips with 'Rosy Amber' and brushed her hair. Whether it was due to being sprinkled with champagne or because of the chlorine she could not decide, but her corn-blonde urchin cut felt like fuse wire.

She checked her wristwatch. Damn. She was now almost ten minutes late and had still to locate the required suite of offices.

After consulting the cleaning women, who had become busy in the lift, she trekked off down what seemed like miles of corridors until she reached glass swing doors emblazoned with the gold-etched words 'Warwick Group'. Both the reception area and the secretary's room to where she was directed were elegantly decorated with neutral cream walls and carpet, offset by richly coloured curtains and upholstery in dark green and magenta. Solid walnut desks and bookshelves gave a feel of bygone years, while the only contemporary note was struck by a cool white computer.

'I'm Jessica Pallister from Citadel Security and I have an appointment with Sir Peter Warwick,' she informed the secretary, who was a bustling middle-aged brunette.

'I'll tell him you're here,' the woman said, with a smile, and disappeared through a connecting door. 'He's not quite ready and asks if you would kindly wait a few minutes,' she reported, coming back. 'Please, take a seat. I must collect a fax,' she continued, hurrying towards the outer door. 'Do excuse me.'

Grateful that her lack of punctuality had been of no consequence, Jess sat down. As she waited, she recapped on the few facts which Kevin had been given about the job. It seemed that Sir Peter had received a note which threatened the safety of an associate who was involved in the construction of a hotel which the Warwick Group were building in Mauritius. A female relative of the person was also at risk and they wished to discuss the employment of two bodyguards, one a woman, initially for a period of three months.

'All the guys are tied up today, but this is just an exploratory talk,' her brother had said, 'so we can decide who goes with you later.'

'*If* I go,' she had pointed out.

Working on an island in the middle of the Indian Ocean would put her way beyond Roscoe Dunbar's reach, Jess reflected, which was a plus. But, on the minus side, whilst blue skies, swaying palms and silver-white beaches had a glamorous spin and were fine on holiday, as a three-month working environment they could become repetitive. Boring. Dull. Yet the bottom line was that after almost five years of shooting off here, there and everywhere on the spur of the moment she had had enough.

She frowned down at her ankle-booted feet. She wanted to stay home, pick up the threads with old friends and concentrate on her painting. This morning she had been all set to announce the decision which, although reached on the spur of the moment, had been building for a long time and cut loose, but Kevin had had his say first. And because she had idolised him from being a tiny girl—as she idolised her other two brothers, Jess thought wryly— she had fallen in with his wishes and agreed to consider the job. Though only consider.

All of a sudden, she tilted her head. The secretary could not have closed the connecting door properly for it had sprung open and through the gap she could hear voices. A trio of male voices. Two of them were low and indecipherable, but the third was plummily, youthfully strident and rang out.

'I believe it's for real and I insist we take precautions, for our protection as well as yours,' the voice said. 'But don't fret, you're not going to be landed with two hulking brutes of ex-boxers, because one of them is a woman.'

Jess sat straighter. They were discussing security. One of the other men spoke earnestly and in what could be recognised as objection, then the ringing voice intruded.

'Ease up, Lorcan. I'm sure your idea of an Amazon who splits bricks with her bare hands and has hairs sprouting from her chin is way off the mark,' it said, and its owner guffawed.

Her hazel eyes burned. Whoever Lorcan was, he had a vivid and insulting imagination!

More indecipherable conversation followed, with the third man joining in, and again the strident voice sounded.

'Let's bring Miss Pallister through and—'

'You have this all fixed?' the objector demanded, his voice lifting in protest, but the connecting door had already been swung open and a baby-faced young man was strolling out.

With gelled fair hair slicked back from his brow and wearing a pearl-grey designer suit, grey shirt, white tie and white leather shoes, he had the self-satisfied air of someone who considered himself to be a cool dude.

Jess rose from her chair. 'Hello.'

Taking a deep drag on the cheroot which he held between two fingers, the young man looked her up and down.

'Gerard Warwick, delighted to meet you,' he murmured, with a smile which was a touch too smooth, a touch too intimate, and, hooking an arm around her shoulders, he steered her with him into the adjoining office. 'See, Lorcan,' he said triumphantly, and indicated a portly, silver-haired man in his sixties, who was seated behind a leather-topped desk. 'My father, Sir Peter.'

'Good afternoon,' Jess said, smiling, and when the business tycoon came round to greet her she shook his hand and introduced herself.

Her smile and introduction were automatic. All she could focus on was the fact that Lorcan, the man whom she had just passed and who had also risen to his feet, was the man from the lift. Though she ought to have guessed, she thought sourly. That 'hairs on her chin' remark could only have come from him!

CHAPTER TWO

SIR PETER thanked her for responding to his call at such short notice, which allowed Jess to apologise for her casual appearance.

'You look charming, my dear,' he declared, with a benign and patently sincere smile. 'May I introduce Lorcan Hunter?' he continued. 'Lorcan is a highly esteemed and much sought-after architect, and we're fortunate that he's building us the most magnificent hotel village in Mauritius.'

She held out her hand. 'Good afternoon.'

After a millisecond's hesitation, when she wondered if he might refuse, her erstwhile victim shook it. His grip was firm and brief. It had occurred to her that it might also be sticky, but it was not. He, too, appeared to have diverted into a bathroom, for his dark hair was neatly combed and no tissue speckles marred the navy pinstriped splendour of his suit. In fact, the only visible evidence of the champagne fiasco was the slightly marinated appearance of his right sleeve.

'You're a bodyguard?' he said, as if not sure whether to howl with derision or bang his head hard against the wall.

'I am.'

'Amazing, isn't it? One false move and you're mincemeat. Isn't that right?' enquired Gerard, and gave another loud guffaw.

Jess's teeth ground together. Whenever she revealed her occupation it invariably evoked a chorus of amused astonishment and puerile jokes, in particular from men. Because she was young and blonde and shapely they seemed to regard her as a comic-cuts Killer Bimbo, and she had grown tired of it.

'I'm meaner than I look,' she said crisply.

Lorcan Hunter fixed her with piercing blue eyes. 'That I do not doubt. You're a whizz at the unexpected attack?' he enquired.

'I have my moments,' she replied, silently defying him to tell his companions about their earlier meeting, which would be embarrassing and could damage her credibility.

'You make grown men cower?'

'From time to time.'

'And put your life and limb at risk?'

She recalled his fury in the lift. 'It can happen, though I always emerge intact,' she said, gazing steadily back.

'How about damage control?'

Her chin firmed. 'I do my best.'

As if sensing something hidden beneath their by-play and resenting it, Gerard placed his hand on her arm. 'Let's sit down,' he said, drawing her with him onto a small upright sofa, while his father returned behind the desk and Lorcan Hunter sat in a wing chair.

At the rub of the young man's thigh against hers, Jess eased away. She did not care for his touchy-feely familiarity nor for the pungent reek of his cheroot, which smelled like a fusion of burnt treacle, drains and sweat-soaked socks.

'To bring you up to speed, Miss Pallister,' Sir Peter said, passing her a sheet of paper, 'this arrived in the post this morning.'

Made up from stuck-on printed words which had been cut from a newspaper, the note read:

> So you think you can outwit me. Big mistake. Your hotel in Mauritius will never be completed. If Hunter returns to the island, he and his precious brunette are doomed to disappear.

'Do you have any idea who might've sent this?' Jess enquired. 'And why?'

Sir Peter hesitated. 'No. The envelope bore a London postmark, but that doesn't mean anything.'

'Come on, Pa,' Gerard protested. 'Charles Sohan is responsible.'

'You mean Charles Sohan of the Sohan hotel chain?' she asked.

'The same. He and my father are rivals.'

Cosmopolitan and commercially shrewd, Charles Sohan owned luxury hotels all over the world. She had stayed in the New York Sohan once when she had been guarding an Arabian princess, Jess remembered, and been most impressed. Her brow crinkled. Whilst her only knowledge of the hotelier came from the media, to her it seemed unlikely that if he wished to launch an attack he would do so in such a petty, melodramatic and hackneyed way.

'But sending something like this is so amateurish. It's not Charles's style at all,' Sir Peter protested, echoing her thoughts.

'The note is a hoax dreamed up by some airhead who wants to cause trouble,' Lorcan Hunter declared, 'and isn't worth bothering about.' Ice-cool blue eyes met hers. 'The last thing I need is a couple of bodyguards lurking in the background.'

Jess gave a narrow smile. 'You're mistaken, Mr Hunter,' she said. 'We do not lurk. We blend seamlessly and unobtrusively into a client's habitat.'

'Not into mine,' he rapped.

She moved her shoulders. 'So be it.'

She had decided that if there was a snag she would refuse the assignment and there was one crucial snag—him. Three months in his company were unlikely to be dull, yet they would be intensely trying on the nerves. Everyone else she had looked after had been grateful—a shadow crossed her face: sometimes *too* grateful—and she was damned if she would be an unwelcome guest.

Gerard shone a soothing, slightly oily smile. 'We're only thinking of your safety,' he told him.

'I realise that, but I would've appreciated it if you'd consulted me before bringing Miss Pallister here today,' the architect said, and gave a noticeably irritated tweak at his damp sleeve. 'It would've saved a lot of hassle.'

'No hassle. It's been my pleasure,' Jess said sweetly, and received a stony glare in reply. She turned to Gerard. 'Have you notified the police?'

He shook his head. 'Any danger would be on Mauritius.'

'Even so, if you believe the threat is genuine—'

'It isn't,' Lorcan interjected.

'It could be,' stated Gerard. 'Yes, Pa?'

His father shifted uneasily in his chair. 'I can't decide, but whoever composed the note knows about Lorcan working on the hotel and his personal arrangements—'

'And if there's doubt it pays to be cautious, though we don't need to bother the police at this stage,' the young man declared, taking over the proceedings again. '"Precious brunette" seems an unusual phrase. Has Sohan ever described Harriet like that?'

'Yes, he has,' Lorcan replied. 'She went with me to his office once and now when we meet it's how he refers to her. But we meet in public, so any number of people could've overheard.'

Sir Peter frowned. 'I can understand your not wishing to be guarded, but you wouldn't want to take even the slightest risk of Harriet getting hurt.'

A nerve pulsed in his temple. 'Good grief, no,' he said sharply.

Presumably the 'precious' Harriet who was to accompany him to Mauritius was his wife, Jess mused— or perhaps a live-in lover. A man like Lorcan Hunter would have his pick of women, so the brunette was bound to be some svelte beauty who dressed in style— she glanced down at her tunic and leggings—whatever the occasion. And whose face never flushed bright red, even if she ran the marathon in the Olympics.

'Harriet is—Mrs Hunter?' she enquired, thinking that she hated the woman already.

'Sorry? No. The reference is to my daughter.' The nerve throbbed again in his temple. 'I'm a widower.'

'So, to be on the safe side, you need someone to watch over her,' Sir Peter said. 'And Gerard thought that if it was a young lady no one would suspect her presence.' He smiled at Jess. 'People will believe you're an au pair or perhaps Lorcan's girlfriend.'

'No, thanks,' the architect said brusquely.

Jess's spine stiffened. She had been about to object to the second description herself, but she saw no reason for him to be so anti!

'OK, we forget the whole idea of bodyguards,' Gerard declared, with a careless wave of his cheroot. He smiled at her through clouds of cloying smoke. 'Sorry you've had a wasted journey.'

'It isn't a problem,' she replied, thinking that for someone who, minutes ago, had been insisting on taking precautions he had undergone a swift change of mind. Yet perhaps Lorcan Hunter was getting a long way up his nose, too?

'We won't forget it,' Sir Peter declared, suddenly sitting up straight and taking charge. 'I'm willing to accept that you prefer to take care of yourself, Lorcan, but I still believe we should consider protection for Harriet. It's another week until you return to Mauritius so there's no need to make a final decision until then, but I'd like her and Miss Pallister to meet. To see if they get along together, if needs be. Do you have any experience of four-year-olds?' he asked her.

She shook her head. Two of her brothers had children, but they were still only babies. 'None.'

'Harriet is four and a quarter,' Lorcan said, and grinned. 'She considers the quarter is of the utmost importance.'

Jess stared. It was the first time he had smiled and it transformed him. His blue eyes had warmed and sparkled, and attractive little dents had appeared in his cheeks. When he relaxed, he *was* handsome. Her gaze fixed on his mouth. Several years ago, she had illustrated book jackets and Lorcan Hunter had the mouth of a hero. His upper lip was thin and sculpted, the lower sensually full. It was a mouth which any artist would drool over. A mouth which ought to be cast in bronze.

'Do you have an hour or two to spare?' Sir Peter enquired. 'Do you have the rest of the afternoon free, Miss Pallister?' he said, and Jess realised, with a start, that he was talking to her.

She sprang back to attention. 'Um—yes,' she replied.

The businessman spoke to Lorcan. 'Then perhaps they could meet this afternoon? You mentioned how you'd brought Harriet up to London with you today to see your folks, so it would seem the perfect opportunity.'

A beat went by before he nodded. 'Whatever you wish.'

Jess frowned. Instead of concocting some polite excuse, turning down the assignment and walking away, she had allowed herself to be drawn in. Though only for the next couple of hours. The architect's hesitation had made it plain that he had agreed to the meeting to oblige his paymaster and was merely going through the motions. And if she went through the motions, too, it would burnish the name of Citadel Security and could persuade Sir Peter to use them should his company require a bodyguard—or hotel guards or mobile patrols or closed circuit TV systems—at some time in the future. Which would delight her brothers.

'You said you didn't tell your parents about the threat, Lorcan, and we don't want to alarm them or Harriet unnecessarily,' the older man went on, 'but I'm sure you can come up with a reason for the introduction.' Rising to his feet, he held out his hand. 'Thank you for your time and your trouble, Miss

Pallister. We'll be in touch with your office to advise them of what action we decide to take, in a few days.'

Ten minutes later, Jess was seated beside Lorcan Hunter in his black Alfa Romeo coupé heading out of Central London and north towards Hampstead Garden Suburb where, he had told her, his parents lived in a small private retirement community.

'So,' she said, 'what role do you wish me to play in this charade?'

He shot her a look. 'Charade?' he repeated cautiously.

'I'm well aware that we're engaged in an exercise in futility because you intend to veto the bodyguard idea, come hell or high water. Yes?'

'Yes,' he agreed. 'I see no need for one.'

'Your choice,' she said. 'So, who am I supposed to be?'

He frowned, thinking. 'Before I formed my own company I was with an international design firm called the Dowling Partnership, working first here and then in the States—'

'Which explains the American twang,' Jess cut in.

'I lived there for several years.'

'It's a super country.'

He nodded. 'It has a lot going for it. How about we say you were a colleague at Dowling's London office?' he went on. 'We met by chance in the street today and you said you'd like to meet Harriet?'

'OK, but—'

'But, what?' he enquired, when she paused.

'Whilst you may consider your daughter to be the best thing since hole-in-the-wall cash dispensers, the only reason a single woman would show such an interest in her would be because she's interested in *you.*' Jess offered him a sunny smile. 'A bizarre concept, I know, but such are the foibles of human nature.'

'You're good at the smartarse comment, Miss Pallister,' he remarked, 'but do you have a better idea?'

'No. I was just pointing out—'

'Then we'll stick with it.'

'Yes, sir. If we're supposed to be one-time colleagues you ought to call me Jess. Short for Jessica,' she told him.

'And it's Lorcan,' he said, a mite reluctantly.

She angled him a look. 'Lorc for short?'

'Only if you're a dear, dear friend,' he said grittily.

'But I don't fit into that category?'

'Not quite.'

'You don't believe Charles Sohan has any connection with the note?' she asked as they skirted the grassy area of Regent's Park and sped up past Lord's cricket ground.

'None. Granted, he and Sir Peter are in competition, and Sohan was eager for me to build him a flagship hotel in Mauritius, but—'

'Why Mauritius?' Jess interrupted.

'Because he originally comes from the island. Around seventy per cent of the population are of Indian extraction, mainly descended from labourers who went there to work in the sugar plantations.'

'And the other thirty per cent?'

'Creoles, Franco-Mauritians and Chinese. When Charles Sohan discovered I'd been engaged to design a hotel complex for the Warwick Group, he immediately offered to double my fee,' Lorcan continued, 'and later to treble it. I refused. Although I'd barely started, it wouldn't have been ethical to pull out.'

'Mr Sohan was annoyed?'

'Hopping mad. Apparently he'd been on the point of contracting me himself and he swore that Sir Peter must've found out and sneaked in first. But he's not the type to seek revenge and, besides, he has a soft spot for Harriet.'

'Sir Peter believes that although the note threatens you and your daughter it's intended to hit at him,' Jess said, 'but it could also be hitting against you. Is there anyone you know who might bear a grudge?'

He shook his head. 'I don't have any enemies—or, at least, none that I'm aware of. But the note is mischief-making,' he dismissed.

'It was still sent for a reason. You may not have enemies as such, but there could be people you've annoyed,' she continued, and skewered him with a look. 'For example, people whom you've shouted at or blamed for something which was beyond their control.'

His fingers tightened around the steering wheel. 'OK, OK, I lost my cool in the lift. But when Gerard rang this morning to say there'd been a death threat against Harriet and me he made it sound so imminent, so serious that it scared the—it wound me up,' he adjusted, 'which was no doubt what the guy intended.' Drawing the coupé to a halt at traffic lights, he turned to face her. 'I reacted with less grace than I should've done. Will you forgive me?'

'You aren't going to grovel?' Jess enquired, for his apology had been clipped.

'I never grovel to anyone,' he replied. 'However, in this instance I do acknowledge that I was less tolerant than I should've been. So?'

She made him wait for a long moment. 'I forgive you, Lorcan.'

'Thanks.'

'Now you can see the funny side?'

The green light shone and he accelerated away from the junction. 'Don't push it, Jess,' he said.

'Why would Gerard want to wind you up?' she enquired as they motored along. 'In my work I've shared all kinds of confidences with all kinds of people and I can be trusted,' she told him. 'I won't blab.'

He subjected her to a discerning look, then nodded, accepting her assurance. 'The guy'd enjoy winding me up because he resents my friendship with his father, plus he feels he should've been consulted about the designing of the hotel.'

'Gerard is an architect, too?' she said, in surprise.

'No. He started to study architecture, but thanks to dabbling in drugs he got himself thrown out of college halfway through the course. He claims he would've sailed through his finals with flying colours, though whether that's true is anyone's guess.'

'Your guess is no?'

'My guess is that the guy has difficulty walking and chewing gum at the same time,' he said succinctly. 'However, this doesn't stop him from thinking he should be running the show in Mauritius and not me. When he visited the site a month ago, he made that abundantly clear.'

'Sir Peter let him run the show earlier,' Jess observed. 'Most of the time.'

'That's because he's his only child and his weak spot. Sir Peter's wife disappeared with some local heart-throb when Gerard was a few months old, so there's always been just the two of them. I understand that when he was a kid he gave him everything he wanted and by the time it dawned that he could be raising a monster he was halfway there.'

'Is Gerard still on drugs?'

He shook his head. 'After the trouble with the college his father halved his allowance, which persuaded him to kick the habit, though now there're rumours he gets his highs from gambling, plus he's a heavy drinker. And he runs around with a very flaky crowd. But Sir Peter's involving him more and more in the business in the hope that he'll develop a taste for hard graft and take over when he retires.'

'Gerard doesn't come over as the hard graft type,' Jess said.

'Anything but. You don't come over as a bodyguard,' Lorcan remarked, and slid her a look. 'Shouldn't they have hair-trigger reflexes?'

'My reflexes are excellent,' she protested. 'All right, when the champagne exploded—'

'You screwed up.'

'Well, maybe, but—'

'There's no "maybe" about it. You made a total, full-blown, unmitigated mess of things.'

Jess glared. There was a gleam in his blue eyes which said he was deliberately riling her—and enjoying himself.

'The reason I wasn't as alert as I should've been was that today nothing's gone right,' she informed him huffily. 'So I was distracted, and a little slower off the mark and—'

'You're premenstrual?' Lorcan suggested, when she sought around for another excuse. 'I believe there're some excellent remedies for PMT on the market.'

'I am not premenstrual and that is so sexist! But maybe the reason you lost your cool earlier is because you're in the throes of the male menopause?' she said, in a feisty tit-for-tat.

'Who's being sexist now? Though I'm only thirty-seven.'

'Fast approaching forty, which makes you ripe for it. And I was off duty,' Jess completed, with an air of 'so there!'.

'When you're on duty, you have your wits about you and are the mistress of any situation?'

Her jaw jutted. 'I do. I am. Though you'll never experience it.'

'Alas and alack,' he drawled, and turned off the main road and into a quiet tree-lined avenue.

Ahead on the left, a pair of wide wrought-iron gates stood open. Swinging the Alfa Romeo through them, he drove onto a cobbled courtyard which was edged by half a dozen cottage-style houses, each with its own flower-filled front garden. To one side stood a row of garages fronted by a parking bay and here he stopped.

'Daddy!' a child's voice shouted as they climbed out of the car, and Jess saw a little girl with long chestnut curls skipping across the courtyard.

She had big blue eyes and dimpled cheeks which were a straight steal from her father, but was small-boned and delicately built. Wearing a white lace party dress and with a white satin bow tied in her hair, she looked like a miniature angel.

Jess had been on the far side of the coupé, but as she came round the child stopped skipping, stood on one leg and studied her. Her gaze was steely and suspicious. Another inherited trait, she thought wryly.

'Who are you?' the little girl demanded.

'This is Miss Pallister,' Lorcan said.

'Jess,' she amended, 'and you must be Harriet.'

'S'right,' the child agreed, pouting.

He bent to swing her up into his arms. 'Got a kiss for your daddy?'

The pout vanished. 'Lots and lots,' she declared, and began to cover his face with energetic kisses.

Watching on, Jess felt a softening around her heart. There was something poignant about a man bringing up a small child on his own and, whilst Lorcan Hunter seemed the last person to inspire her sympathy, she could not help feeling sorry for him. Sorry that he had lost his wife. Sorry he was a single parent with its accompanying strains and stresses—though perhaps, by now, he had a second Mrs Hunter lined up?

As the kisses ended, Lorcan set his daughter down on her feet and indicated one of the houses. They were walking along the garden path when an old lady in a lilac two-piece and with her fly-away white hair caught back into a bun appeared in the doorway.

'I thought I saw a visitor and what a lovely surprise,' she said, in a soft Irish accent. She smiled at Jess. 'I'm Peg Hunter.'

Smiling back, Jess gave her name. Unlike her son and granddaughter, Peg Hunter displayed an easy warmth and instant friendliness. She also confirmed her hunch that a part of Lorcan's ancestry was derived from the Celtic.

'Do come in,' the old lady entreated, leading the way into a cosy, rather cluttered living room where a spare, distinguished-looking old man was sitting on a sofa reading a newspaper. 'We have a guest, Bob,' she told him.

'This is Jess Pallister who used to work with me long ago at Dowlings,' Lorcan said, introducing her. 'We bumped into each other just now and I've brought her to see Harriet.'

His father greeted her with a smiling hello and everyone sat down.

'When me and Grandma went shopping I had three ice-creams,' Harriet announced, leaning against Lorcan's knees.

As she had idolised her brothers, so Jess recognised that the little girl idolised her father. And as she had not cared for it when her brothers had brought a strange female into the house, so Harriet's gimlet-eyed looks along the sofa showed that she had serious doubts about her presence.

'Three?' Lorcan protested. 'Ma, that's ridiculous. So many times I've—'

'How about making us a cup of tea?' his father suggested.

'Right away,' Peg said. She was halfway to the kitchen when she stopped and turned. 'You asked me to buy Harriet a new dress; do you like it?'

Lorcan frowned at the white lace extravaganza. 'Very nice.'

His reply had been tempered and Jess understood why. The dress was fussy and twee and Shirley Temple. Just the kind of dress which would appeal to an elderly lady, but murder to wash and iron.

'I didn't want it,' piped up Harriet. 'I wanted the blue dress.'

'But, sweetheart, the shop didn't have a blue one in your size,' her grandmother said, 'and this is almost the same.'

The little girl stamped her foot. 'Don't care. I don't like this one.' Squeezing up her face, she forced out a couple of tears. 'I don't like white.'

Replace 'angel' with 'Hell's angel', Jess thought. Though what else could you expect when you considered her genes?

'Don't cry, sweetheart,' Peg appealed, looking as if she might cry herself.

'I hate white! White is stinky!'

'So we'll make it blue,' Jess said.

As if clicked off by a switch, the temper tantrum stopped.

'How?' demanded Harriet.

Standing up, she held out her hand. 'If you come with me to your daddy's car where I left my bag, I'll show you.'

'You need the key,' Lorcan said, lifting a hip and reaching into his pocket. 'Here you are.'

When they returned a few minutes later, Harriet was wearing a pair of swimming goggles. They were blue-tinted goggles.

'My dress is blue now,' she declared, smiling down at the skirt. 'And you're blue, Daddy. And Grandma. And Grandpa. And—'

As the little girl lifted a cushion, turned pages in a book, peered out of the window and happily pronounced everything blue, her grandmother served tea and home-made sponge cake.

'Where do you live, Jess?' Peg enquired pleasantly.

'In Wimbledon.'

'You live alone?'

'Yes, in a small flat. Though my family are nearby so someone's always calling round.'

'Have you ever been married?' the old lady asked.

'No. I was almost engaged once, but I've travelled a lot over the past few years and separations aren't conducive to long-term relationships,' she said ruefully.

'How about a boyfriend now?'

She shook her head.

'So you're fancy-free, just like my son is fancy-free,' Peg said, her smile swinging between the two of them. 'Isn't that nice?'

At the other end of the sofa, Lorcan's grim-faced silence accompanied by a swift gulp of his tea indicated that he was becoming impatient. Jess grinned. As he had riled her and enjoyed himself, so she recognised a chance to have some fun at his expense.

'It was wonderful to meet up after all this time,' she declared. 'Wasn't it, Lorcan?'

A line cut between his brows. 'Yes,' he replied guardedly.

'He's such a friendly, easygoing kind of a guy.' Putting down her teacup, she stretched out a hand and squeezed his knee. 'A poppet.'

For a moment, he seemed about to choke.

'There's always been a rapport between us,' Jess carried on blithely, and shot him a look, pleased by the fire she saw in his eyes. 'A strong one.'

'So you'll be meeting again?' Peg enquired.

'That's up to your son,' she murmured, lowering her gaze and acting coy.

Very deliberately—and as if she might be the carrier of the Black Death or some other lethal and highly contagious disease—Lorcan took hold of her wrist and lifted her hand from his knee. He stood up.

'Time I took Jess home,' he declared.

'Already?' his mother protested.

'I'm afraid so,' she said, taking her cue and rising too. Enough was enough. It would be foolish to overdo things and have him complaining to Sir Peter about her behaviour. 'Thanks for the tea, but I must go.'

Harriet came to stand in front of her. 'Do you want these?' she asked, her eyes bright and anxious behind the goggles.

'No, you can keep them.'

'For ever?'

'For ever and ever,' Jess assured her.

The child gave her a solemn look. 'Thank you.'

Goodbyes were exchanged, Peg expressed the hope that Jess would come again soon, and they took their leave.

'Boy, you're really something,' Lorcan muttered as he unlocked the car.

Jess made innocent eyes at him across the roof. 'I was only adding a little colour.'

'By calling me poppet?'

'You'd have preferred dearest heart?'

'I'd have preferred it if you'd kept your lip buttoned. OK, my mother was grilling you and I apologise for that, but there was no need to give her the wrong idea.'

'The moment she saw me she had the wrong idea. I did warn you.'

'Maybe,' he conceded, 'but now she'll be asking about you for months, because she liked you!'

'I'm a likeable person.'

'Then how come you manage to annoy the hell out of me?' Lorcan enquired.

'It's a gift,' she replied airily, and climbed into the car. 'Please don't bother to drive me home,' Jess said as he swung the coupé out onto the road. 'I can easily take the Underground, so if you'd just run me to the nearest station. It'll be much quicker than driving back through the city and I only have a short walk at the other end.'

'You're sure?'

'Certain.'

'Thanks, I'll do that,' he said. 'It means I can relieve my folks of Harriet and get her home and in bed at a reasonable time.'

'Home is where?'

'West Sussex, and the journey takes around an hour and a half depending on the traffic.'

'You obviously don't have a girlfriend,' she remarked as they turned back onto the main road.

'No. Much to my mother's dismay. But as you travel, so I've moved around in the two years since my wife died, and what with that and caring for Harriet I haven't had the opportunity to embark on a relationship.'

A tightness had entered his voice and when she looked at his profile she saw the nerve pulsing in his temple.

'Nor the inclination?' she asked.

'I have my share of raging hormones,' Lorcan said drily, 'so I guess I'd be open to a torrid affair with no strings attached. But as far as anything serious goes—no. I'm not interested in commitment. Thanks for sidetracking Harriet about the dress,' he went on.

'She can be a little witch at times. And thank you for the goggles. How much did they cost?'

'I don't remember, but put them towards the dry-cleaning of your suit.'

He gave a cryptic smile. 'Will do. I'm also grateful for your co-operation in the charade,' he said as they reached the Underground station. 'Correction, fifty per cent grateful.' Drawing into the kerb, he halted. 'You don't mind missing out on the Mauritius job?'

She shook her head. 'On the contrary, it suits me fine.'

'It does?' he asked, sounding suddenly uncertain.

'My dear Mr Hunter, the last thing I need is three months lurking around *you*,' Jess said, and climbed out of the car and walked away.

CHAPTER THREE

As FAST as suitcases tumbled off the carousel in the arrivals hall at the Sir Seewoosagur Ramgoolam international airport, the jovial Creole porter hauled them back onto it again. The simultaneous arrival of two jumbo jets, combined with slow Passport Control which delayed the claiming of luggage, meant that the circling belt was vastly overloaded.

Jess watched as a heap of miscellaneous Styrofoam parcels jiggled by. Because they had travelled club class their cases were supposed to have been taken off first, yet although Lorcan had all of his stacked on a trolley her two had yet to arrive.

'When can we go?' Harriet asked plaintively.

'Just as soon as the rest of the bags come through,' Lorcan replied, in a voice of sore-tried patience.

'If they came through,' Jess said.

After the twelve-hour flight with an in-transit stop in the Seychelles, all three of them were weary. It had been an early morning departure and a daytime journey, and no one had slept.

Jess circled a look around. A crowded arrivals hall seemed an unlikely place for villains to strike, but she was being paid to be on the alert—and she refused to screw up this time. Her brow creased. Though who or what she was on the alert *for* she did not know. His daughter's ever listening presence had prevented her from asking the architect why, when the job had been cancelled as expected, there had been a last-minute request for her services.

'We'd better make enquiries,' Lorcan said, when most of the cases had been claimed and fresh items were no longer appearing.

Jess wiped a slick of moisture from her brow. Outside the rain was sheeting down and the atmosphere in the hall was as hot and humid as a sauna.

'I suppose so,' she acknowledged.

At a desk on the back wall, an Indian clerk checked the baggage slips stapled to her ticket, made a phone call and reported the damning news that all goods from their plane had been cleared.

'Oh, no!' she groaned.

'Now you must fill in this form and the airline will put the tracing procedure into operation. Most bags are retrieved within a few days,' the clerk told her, with a comforting smile, 'but until then you may buy immediate needs and claim the cost against the allowance.'

By the time they emerged through Customs, the afternoon had slithered into early evening and the airport concourse was almost deserted. A four-wheel drive was parked at the entrance under cover from the rain, with a young man half-asleep inside it.

'Mr Hunter?' he called, rousing himself when he saw them.

He was waiting to deliver the Jeep Cherokee which Lorcan had hired, and after paperwork was completed and the luggage loaded they climbed inside.

'Would you like me to navigate?' Jess asked, eyeing the map of the island which the car hire representative had handed to her.

Lorcan started the engine. 'No need, thanks. The house is just a few miles from the hotel site, so I know my way.'

'My daddy's been here before,' Harriet said importantly, from where she was buckled into the rear seat. 'Three times. When he came my grandma and grandpa looked after me. And Senga. Senga was my nanny, but she's gone back to Scotland to get married. And now you're going to look after me.'

Jess darted a glance at her chauffeur. The supposed reason for her presence was just one of a whole raft of questions which she needed to ask and matters which they had to discuss. Soonest.

She smiled at the child. 'And Naseem,' she said, referring to the local woman whom Lorcan had told her he had employed as a housekeeper-cum-childminder.

'S'right,' Harriet agreed, and smiled back.

The little girl's original suspicion had gone and she was prepared to be friendly. This could be thanks to the goggles, which had been brought with other treasured possessions in her haversack and which continued to cast a spell, or, more realistically, Jess thought, it was because Harriet had marked her down as paid help. When her status had been unsure she had threatened—who was this strange lady with her daddy?—but now she had become acceptable. Her thought train jumped track. What was the threat which she had been recruited to deflect?

When they first left the airport Jess kept a discreet check to see that no particular vehicle appeared to be trailing them, but after a few miles she gave up. They were almost the only people out on the road. Besides, the relentless tropical rain would deter ninety-nine per cent of kidnappers, she reasoned—and she would take her chance with the remainder. Her gaze went to the strong hands which so deftly controlled the steering wheel and down to the gear-changing flex of a muscled thigh. Though it would take a determined gang to remove his beloved daughter when the well-built Lorcan Hunter was around.

She peered out through the window. The continuous driving rain had made it impossible to see anything of the island when their plane had landed, and now all she could make out were rolling fields where sugar cane had been harvested and the occasional blurred outline of a sharp, rugged mountain. Mauritius was grey, washed of colour, wet.

What was she doing here? Jess wondered. As her luggage seemed to have remained at home, wouldn't she have done better to have stayed home, too?

'Sorry, Kev, I'm not interested,' she had said yesterday morning, when her brother had rung to announce that the Warwick Group had performed an eleventh-hour about-turn and wished to use her. Yet within minutes she had allowed him to talk her into it.

The windscreen-wipers moved in a rhythmic swish-swish. Why had she agreed? Was it a case of old habits dying hard—though she had insisted that this was her *very last* assignment—or because she had recognised that a stay in the sun did have its uses? Tropical island pictures were perennially popular and during her residence she would be able to build up a portfolio of local scenes. A hopefully saleable and lucrative portfolio.

Jess sighed. Whatever the reason, she had committed herself to joining forces with a man who was iron-willed and bolshie. And a man who, whilst he must have sanctioned her employment, still resented it.

Lorcan Hunter's resentment was subtle. From meeting her at the airport, he had acted the civilised adult and been polite, amiable and—yes—at times even charming. Yet although they had chatted together and laughed she had been aware of a tightness within him. A basic irritation. He did not want her here disrupting his life and, whilst her presence might be necessary and he was currently co-operating, she sensed there would be battles ahead.

'Don't worry about it,' Lorcan said, all of a sudden.

Jolted from her musing, she shot him a startled look. 'Sorry?'

'I'm sure your cases will turn up soon.'

'Oh . . . yes,' Jess agreed, thinking that if she was destined to do battle with him she would survive. He might be a cussed individual, but she could be tough-minded, too.

'Even if you do seem to be accident-prone,' he added.

Recognising a reference to the champagne debacle, she flashed a synthetic smile. 'It only happens when I'm with you.'

'You'll have a change of clothes in your hand luggage to tide you over?'

Visualising the sports bag which she had brought, she shook her head. 'No.'

'But if you're travelling long haul it's common sense to carry a spare set. I do. I have.'

'Don't you ever get just the teeniest weeniest bit sick of always being right?' Jess enquired sweetly.

Lorcan's mouth quirked. 'Nope.'

'Amazing. Even if I'd thought about it, which I didn't,' she said, 'there wouldn't have been room for spare clothes because my bag is full of painting gear.'

'You must've brought one heck of an amount.'

'Enough sketchpads, brushes, water colours, pencils, pens and inks to last me for three months.'

His brows lifted. 'Sounds like you're keen.'

'I am.' She looked down at the white-on-white long-sleeved body which she wore, her slim-fitting black skirt, her black-stockinged legs. 'But I'm even keener to find a dress shop.'

Because she had felt like a slob at their first meeting, Jess had been determined to be elegant the second time around. The previous evening, she had applied a face pack, waxed her legs and colour co-ordinated her finger and toenails with 'Pearl Sirocco' lacquer. And that morning she had swept into the airport with her hair blow-dried into a silky blonde cap and teased into wisps across her brow, her face painstakingly made up and clad in a smart black suit with a sculpted high-necked jacket and high heels.

Her efforts might have been a touch over the top, but they were worthwhile. Lorcan Hunter had looked, done a double take, and looked again. He had seemed bewitched, until he had remembered that La Stupenda was the pesky bodyguard. But after he had brought himself to heel other admiring male glances had swung her way. Glances which, satisfyingly, she knew he had noticed.

However, her elegance had its drawbacks. At the airport, she had been one of a chic minority amongst the ubiquitous jeans and anoraks, and now... Jess shifted and felt her back sticking clammily to the seat. Before they'd landed, Lorcan had shed his sweater to reveal a short-sleeved navy shirt which, worn with stone-coloured cotton chinos, conceded to the climate. She had removed her jacket, but the tight white body, hip-hugging skirt and nylon stockings meant that despite the Cherokee's air-conditioning she was bathed in steam heat.

The white body was clinging to her damp skin, outlining the high curve of her breasts and—she abruptly realised—drawing her chauffeur's attention. Jess sat very still. The stroke of his eyes seemed as tactile as the stroke of fingers and she felt her nipples pinch and tighten. She gulped in a breath. He was arousing her with just a look. How could he do that?

'Is the house which you've rented near a town? Close to shops?' she rattled off. 'Because I'd like to buy a change of clothes as soon as I can tomorrow.'

'No, it's on the outskirts of a small fishing village,' Lorcan said, frowning as though being bewitched by her again had been an irritating—and curious—lapse. 'There are a few shops, though I'm afraid I couldn't say what they are. But until you get fixed up you can wear one of my shirts and a pair of shorts. They'll be far too big, but you can hoist up the shorts with a belt.'

Jess shot him a glance. The offer of his clothes seemed surprisingly free and easy.

'You're trying to impress me with your kindness,' she said.

'Wait until you see my gear,' he responded. 'It's nothing special and I may keep the best for myself and restrict you to the rag-bag end.'

'Gee, thanks.'

'Are we nearly there?' Harriet asked as they turned off the metalled road and onto a muddy track.

'Soon. In about ten minutes, fishface,' Lorcan told her. 'The house is an old colonial bungalow,' he continued, negotiating the Jeep through a deep water-filled pothole. 'It backs onto fields and is close to the beach and a short walk from the village.'

'I'm going to go to play-school in the village,' Harriet said. She hesitated, and when Jess turned she saw that her lower lip was trembling. 'I don't think I'll like it.'

'It'll be fun,' she said encouragingly.

'You'll love it,' Lorcan declared.

'I might not,' the little girl said, and put her thumb in her mouth and sucked earnestly.

A couple of miles later, the dirt track smoothed into a surfaced road again and shapes of buildings began to appear through the curtain of rain. Jess peered out. She saw flat-roofed breeze-block houses with ramshackle gardens where large cacti were strung with sodden washing, a Chinese restaurant, a jarring glass and chrome space-age-style bar and a row of shops. The shops were shuttered, but so far as she could tell there was no dedicated clothing store.

A long bend took them out of the village. To the right, through casuarina trees, were glimpses of a grey swelling sea, while on the left woebegone goats munched in a water-logged meadow. At the end of the meadow was a lane. Turning into it, Lorcan sped up past more affluent houses until they reached two stately dripping palms which stood like sentinels at the entrance to a gravelled drive.

'This is it,' he said.

Beyond a circular lawn stood a wide double-fronted wooden bungalow with an all-round veranda. Painted Wedgwood blue, it had white window shutters and a pretty white decorative valence edging the roof. Even in the rain, which had slackened into a steady drizzle, it was a gracious building and would, Jess decided, be an ideal subject for a water colour.

Lorcan drew to a stop beside the short flight of steps which led up to the white-glossed front door. 'Naseem promised to leave the keys under the plant pot,' he said, indicating a terracotta tub which spilled with crimson bougainvillea.

'She isn't here?' she asked.

'No. I agreed she need only come in in the mornings until we arrived. Though as from tomorrow it's all day.'

'Naseem doesn't live in?' she said, frowning. 'I realise you didn't actually say, but—well, I assumed she did.'

'Does it make a difference?' he enquired.

Jess unbuckled her seat belt. 'None.'

The bungalow had spacious lofty rooms, tall, slim windows and ceiling fans. A wide central hall divided it into two distinct areas, with what Lorcan showed her and Harriet were the living room, a study and eat-in kitchen to one side, while three bedrooms lay on the other.

'I thought this could be yours,' he said, opening the door onto a square room which overlooked the rain-sleeked greenery of a fenced and private back garden. 'I'm opposite and Harriet is next to me.'

With white voile curtains, white cotton-twist rugs on the highly polished floorboards and a big old-fashioned wardrobe and dresser, the bedroom was simple but comfortable. Off it was an up-to-date yet period-flavour bathroom which included a glassed-in shower cubicle, huge claw-footed bath tub and basin with gleaming brass taps.

'Fine,' she agreed.

'I don't like this house,' Harriet announced belligerently as they went back into the hall. 'There's no proper carpet and the furniture's all old and stinky. Wommie doesn't like it, either.'

'The house is lovely,' Lorcan said, his voice gentle. 'You'll think so in the morning after you've had a good night's sleep.'

'I'll think it's horrid!'

'Who's Wommie?' Jess asked.

Pushing out her chin and her stomach, Harriet looked defiant. A pint-sized warrior. 'My friend.'

'Her pretend friend,' Lorcan said, with a weary roll of his eyes. 'How about a bowl of cornflakes before you go to bed?' he asked his daughter. 'I arranged for Naseem to buy some specially.'

The little girl nodded. Her rebellion seemed to have used up her last ounce of energy and all of a sudden she was exhausted.

'I could give Harriet her cornflakes while you unload your luggage,' Jess suggested.

He smiled gratefully. 'Thanks.'

Like her bathroom, the kitchen had recently been refurbished and was well equipped. She found the cornflakes with other groceries in a cool tiled larder, milk in the fridge, and a bowl and spoon in the pine units. All the crockery and cutlery was attractive and clean.

As Harriet was finishing her cereal, Lorcan reappeared. 'We'll skip a bath and put you straight to bed, fishface,' he said, with a look at her drooping eyelids. 'Would you like something to eat?' he asked Jess.

'No, thanks, I had more than enough with the meals on the plane.'

'Likewise,' he said.

'But I will have a coffee. Can I make you one?'

He shook his head. 'I'll have something stiffer a bit later,' he said, and, scooping up the unresisting child, he carried her away.

Jess brewed a mug of instant coffee and sat down at the kitchen table. She had said that Naseem's non-residence made no difference, she thought, but it did. Due to all the rush of packing, arranging to leave her flat unoccupied and buying traveller's cheques, there had been no time to consider the mechanics of life with Lorcan Hunter, even accompanied by a house-keeper, and now she felt . . . edgy.

She sipped at her coffee. Although most of the people she had protected had been female, she had guarded males, yet on those occasions she had always stayed in hotels. Her work had never involved her in living with a man alone and in such close proximity. Indeed, the only time she had co-habited had been with her would-be fiancé. Then she had revelled in finding a naked Adonis in the shower, waking up with a muscular arm wrapped around her, sharing kisses as they passed—or she had at the beginning. But the prospect of co-habiting with Lorcan Hunter was causing havoc in the pit of her stomach.

Think straight, Jess instructed herself. Uncross the wires. This co-habitation is strictly business, strictly platonic, plus it comes with strong reservations on both sides.

The basically hostile Mr Hunter was not going to creep into her room in the dead of night and attempt to seduce her; though even if he did she was well able to protect herself.

'Harriet's already asleep,' Lorcan reported, appearing in the doorway. He beckoned. 'Come along.'

Jess stood up. 'Where to?'

'My room.'

She had started to walk towards him, but her footsteps faltered. 'Your room?' she repeated, looking at him with wide hazel eyes.

Her thoughts ran wild. They had barely arrived...but with her clinging clothes she had tweaked his libido...and the architect would go all out for what he wanted and not waste time...and if he was as assured sexually as he was in every other area he would be a demon lover.

'To take your pick of shirt and shorts,' he said.

Her cheeks flamed. 'Of course,' she mumbled.

What was the matter with her? Jess wondered as she went with him into the hall. She was twenty-eight years old, mature and eminently sensible, so how come she had started to behave like a jittery, fanciful schoolgirl? It must be jet lag.

Unlocking a suitcase, Lorcan took out bundles of clothes and laid them on the bed. 'Help yourself.'

'But keep your sticky fingers off the Armani gear?'

He grinned. 'Armani? Dream on. No, I'm giving you a free run.'

She chose a white short-sleeved shirt, a pair of cream shorts and a narrow black leather belt.

'I'll go and shower and change,' she said. 'And then I'd like us to get a game plan organised and the ground rules fixed.'

He nodded. 'I've unpacked Harriet's things, but I've still to see to my own. So give me half an hour.'

In her room, Jess peeled off the suffocating body, skirt and stockings. Her white satin bra and briefs followed. An air-conditioner was fixed high on one wall and she stood naked in its cooling flow. She raised her arms. What a relief!

Fortunately her toilet bag had been squeezed in with her painting things at the last minute, so when she showered she was able to shampoo her hair.

As she dried herself on one of the thick white towels which had been provided, Jess looked at her reflection in the mirror. The nipples which had risen earlier in such flagrant arousal spread in dark brown circles against the pale cream of her skin. Rubbing the towel over her torso, she drew it up between her breasts. As it grazed across one damp peak, a quiver shot through her.

It was a long time since she had made love, Jess brooded. And she was a healthy young woman and her body had needs. She released a breath. Being with Lorcan Hunter was making her woefully aware of those needs.

Pulling on her underwear, she stepped into the shorts and belted them around her waist. The shirt was left loose over them. As she fastened the buttons, she frowned. To be wearing Lorcan's clothes—sharing them—seemed alarmingly personal. She could not help but think of how the shirt which had once covered his body was now covering hers, and that the cotton which had slid against his naked skin touched her skin.

Jess towelled her hair and in a few minutes it was dry. All her life she had had long blonde tresses which had swung around her shoulders, but a couple of years

ago—on the day her live-in relationship had been mu-
tually declared defunct—she had marched into a salon
and demanded that they be ruthless with the scissors.

When she had seen her hair dropping all around,
a wave of panic had swept over her. What had she
done? But she had quickly realised the joy of being
able to get out of bed in the morning and not worry.
She flicked at the fringe which skimmed her brows.
And it was a sensuous feeling to run your fingers
through your own hair.

Barefoot, she padded into the kitchen to check that
the back door and windows were secure, and went on
to inspect the window in the study. Next came the
living room. As she had been showering it had grown
dark and she switched on the lights. A golden glow
shone from two chandeliers, illuminating an over-
stuffed sofa in poppy-printed batik and a pair of
matching armchairs. Between them a rectangular
coffee-table sat four-square on a green rug. A large
sideboard stood against one wall, while bookshelves
filled another. Like most rented accommodation the
bungalow tended towards the spartan, and the sideboard and shelves were bare.

Jess walked to the open window. The rain had
stopped and a pale melon moon and a million stars
shone in a black velvet sky. She sniffed the air. It
smelled of fresh washed earth and fragrant blossoms.
She was idly speculating on the history of the house
and who had been its original owners, when a floor-
board creaked.

Swivelling, she found Lorcan standing in the
doorway. He had a broad shoulder leant against the
frame and seemed to have been there for a while. He
was frowning. Frowning at her.

'You can't expect me to be a glamour puss twenty-four hours a day,' she protested, with a downward glance at the shirt and shorts.

He straightened. 'You look great. I heard you walking around,' he said, his tone brusque.

'I was checking that the house is secure,' Jess explained, now wondering if he thought she had been prying. 'Is Harriet's bedroom window locked?'

'I think so.'

'You're not sure?'

'Not a hundred per cent, but no one's going to break in tonight.'

'How do you know?' she enquired.

'I don't,' Lorcan said impatiently. 'So if you want to check that, too—go ahead.'

'I will,' she declared, and marched out past him.

He might be prepared to take chances; she was not.

The child's room was dark, the only light coming from the moon which shone in through the top half of the window where the upper shutters had been left open. Tiptoeing across, Jess checked the window catch. It was locked. As she made her way back alongside the bed, she stopped. Harriet's thumb had dropped out of her mouth and she was curled up in a ball—a deep-asleep puppy in Winnie the Pooh pyjamas.

Poor little girl, she thought. She has no mother to love, nor to love her and yell at her, and experience the pleasure of watching her grow up. She said a silent prayer. Please, *please* let Harriet like the play-school.

'Happy now?' Lorcan enquired, when she returned to the living room.

'Yes.' Jess paused. 'It may not seem like it, but I'm here to help, not hinder.'

'OK, but I don't consider there's any need to turn the house into Fort Knox. Let's not get paranoid.'

'I'm not. However, I do take my responsibilities seriously and it pays to be sensible.'

'I guess,' he agreed, and raked a hand back through his thick dark hair. 'I'm going to have a glass of the malt which I bought in duty free. Ditto?'

Although she was not particularly fond of whisky, his suggestion seemed like a peace offering and she was eager to accept a truce.

'I'll have a small one, thanks,' Jess said, 'with the same again of water and ice.'

'Ice in a fine malt? That's sacrilege,' he protested, 'and I don't know if we have ice.'

'There's a full tray in the freezer compartment of the fridge.'

He sent her a long look. 'You appear to have this place already sussed out.'

'Awareness is part of my remit,' she told him.

Lorcan disappeared along the hall to the kitchen, and soon returned carrying two crystal tumblers. He handed one to her. 'You wanted to fix a game plan and ground rules,' he said, levering his long body down into an armchair opposite.

'I do, but first I'd like to know what the second note said.'

'Second note?'

'I assume it had to be another threat which made you decide you needed me. Though perhaps it came in a phone call?'

'There hasn't been another threat, of any kind.' He drank from his glass. 'But I thought that as Sir Peter was keen for Harriet to be guarded I'd go along with it.'

Jess frowned. 'I seem to be missing a step here. You were convinced there wasn't any danger and determined not to have security, regardless of Sir Peter's or anyone else's inclinations. Remember?'

'I don't believe there is any danger, for me. But I guess it makes sense for you to keep watch over Harriet.'

'It doesn't make sense to me,' she retorted, taking a sip of whisky and feeling the alcohol burn a fiery line down her throat. 'The note mentioned the two of you, so either you're both under threat or you're not.'

'I can look after myself,' he said, his tone the equivalent of a brick wall. 'You're here to protect my daughter, period.'

'I'm here to prevent her from being snatched by one of Charles Sohan's minions? But you were adamant that Mr Sohan wouldn't seek revenge and if he's fond of Harriet he's hardly likely to put her into a situation which would distress her, so why—?'

'I changed my mind,' Lorcan said sharply.

'And my presence is a gesture to pacify Sir Peter?'

He frowned down into his whisky. 'More or less.'

Jess prodded at the ice cubes. She barely knew him and was operating on instinct, but his last-minute collapse of resistance did not ring true. It seemed out of character for a man of such determination and strong convictions. So why did he have her in tow?

'If I'm to be fully effective, you have to give me the full facts,' she told him.

'*You* changed your mind. As I recall you were *adamant* that you had no desire to accompany me to Mauritius. It was the last thing you needed and yet here you are.' He nailed her with a look. 'Shall we consider the game plan?'

She sucked at her finger. Perhaps she was wrong and he had reconsidered? After all, the mention in the note of 'precious brunette', a phrase which Charles Sohan used, did seem curious and was a little disturbing.

'Where is the play-school held?' she asked, getting down to business.

'In a church hall beside the harbour.'

'Harriet will attend every day?'

'Five mornings a week, as from tomorrow. In the afternoons she'll either play here at the house or down on the beach. And at the weekends I'll be around—unless some crisis should crop up at work—which means there'll be no need for your surveillance.'

'So I'm to take her to and from school and stand guard while she's there, and look after her in the afternoons?'

'Please.'

Jess took another small drink. 'Presumably you don't want Harriet to realise she could be in danger?'

'No way,' Lorcan said firmly.

'The play-school people will need to be made aware of the reason for my presence, though we can tell them in confidence and without going into detail. However, I don't see why anyone else should know.'

'I agree. I'll come with you to the school tomorrow morning,' he said, 'to make sure everything goes smoothly.'

'OK. Did you tell Harriet that I'm here as a nanny?' she went on.

He nodded. 'It seemed as good an alibi as any. And I told my parents that you'd offered to come in that capacity.'

'They believed you?'

'After the way you so seductively stroked my thigh? I doubt it.'

'I squeezed your knee,' Jess protested. 'Once.'

'No, your fingers slipped upwards. I remember it was most provocative. Hell, you nearly gave me a—'

'My fingers did not slide!' she cut in frantically, and stopped. The twinkle in his blue eyes said that he was baiting her—and she was falling for it. How naïve! 'So your mother suspects ulterior motives?' she asked, aiming for a more even tone.

'She does, and she's delighted,' Lorcan said drily. 'Is being classed as a nanny acceptable?'

'It is, so long as you realise that I'm employed to protect your daughter and not to act as a deputy children's nurse. Which means I don't wash and iron her clothes, or clean her shoes, or— '

'I shan't expect anything like that,' he interrupted. 'Have you been roped in as a children's nurse before?'

'No, because I've never guarded a child before. But a couple of the women I protected tried to use me as a personal maid and general fetch-this, fetch-that dogsbody.'

He grinned. 'Not for long, I imagine?'

'You imagine correctly.'

'What made you decide to become a bodyguard?' he asked.

Jess gave a rueful smile. 'My brothers. I have three. Kevin, who's the boss of Citadel Security, and Paul and Jonathan, who run different parts of the company. I'd planned to make a career in art—'

'So painting isn't just a hobby?'

'No. I studied art at college and when I graduated I landed a job illustrating book jackets. For the first year it was satisfying, but—' she turned down her mouth '—painting to-die-for heroes and beautiful maidens to grace the covers of romantic novels soon becomes a little samey.'

'You had models sitting for you?' Lorcan enquired.

'Sometimes if a publisher wanted an extra special cover they'd wheel in an extra special hunk with the soulful eyes, chiselled jaw and perfect physique of a Calvin Klein men's fragrance ad.'

'But they told you to look in the mirror for the heroine?'

Jess tilted a brow. 'You flatterer, you.'

'Aren't I just? But with cheekbones to hang your hat on—' his eyes fell and lingered '—and that mouth . . .'

'It's too big. Heroines have rosebud mouths. They also have long silken manes and not—' she ruffled her hair '—tomboy crops like this. I'd begun to look for another job in the art line,' she continued, 'when Kevin was asked if he could provide a female body-guard to accompany a ballad singer when she went on tour. He suggested I might like to do it. I wasn't keen, but my other brothers weighed in and pointed out that I'd still be able to draw—much of guarding someone consists of hanging around killing time—and eventually I agreed. It was low-level stuff keeping fans at bay and anything seemed preferable to illustrating another book jacket.'

'Your brothers believed you were capable of looking after the singer—and yourself?'

She nodded. 'When I was a kid I was always desperate to do everything they did, so I'd insisted on going to judo classes and experimented with other martial arts. I also learned to give as good as I got verbally.'

'I've noticed,' Lorcan said.

'If you're outnumbered three to one you either sink or—'

'You grow up to become an exquisite young woman of formidable drive?'

Jess took another sip of whisky. The 'exquisite' pleased her, though she had doubts about the 'formidable'—so she decided to ignore them both.

'After the tour with the singer, Kevin persuaded me to accept other assignments and in time I progressed to high-level work.'

'Which means?'

'Providing protection against stalkers, kidnappers or potential assassins.'

He raised his brows. 'Sounds dangerous. Were you armed?'

'No, because carrying a gun is illegal in the UK—though I do know how to use one. However, I can throw a handy pepper spray, which is illegal, too. But in reality the danger is minimal. I always do my best to keep my "principals" from getting into sticky situations and if there should be problems I attempt to solve them in a peaceful way. A bodyguard is a preventative measure,' she said, 'and usually their presence is enough of a deterrent.'

'Hot damn, so instead of you I could've hired a Dobermann?'

'It wouldn't have been the same.'

'I don't know,' he drawled. 'A bitch with a bite.'

Jess flashed an on-off smile. 'Female bodyguards are a growing trend,' she carried on, 'and they make some of the best. Women are natural observers and unlike many men are not into confrontation.' She paused. 'Nor do they have a five o'clock shadow.'

Lorcan's mouth tweaked. 'You overheard?'

'I did, and you have the wrong perception.'

'I agree.' He leant forward. 'There's not a hair to be seen—unless you had a quick shave earlier?'

'Careful,' she warned. 'I can send you flying at the flick of a wrist.'

'And I thought you were just a slip of a girl.'

Jess groaned. 'That is so corny.'

'Sorry, couldn't resist it.'

'OK, but for the record I'm not a girl. I'm a full-grown woman.'

'That I have noticed, too,' he said, and frowned. He took a drink of his whisky. 'I guess being tall must help in guarding people?'

'Yes, in so much as height bestows a natural authority.'

'You're what—five ten?'

She nodded. 'And well over six foot in my heels.'

'Being tall doesn't bother you?'

'Not now, though when I was growing up I had a real complex about it. For years I towered above the other girls in my class at school and I felt so gangly.'

'Sounds familiar,' Lorcan remarked.

Jess looked at the width of his shoulders and his muscular physique. 'You were a beanpole?'

'A radio mast more like. To finish your story...' he prompted.

'Er—' she realised she was gazing at him again '—I take my painting gear on every assignment and usually manage a fair amount of drawing and painting.'

'You've drawn and painted what?'

'For example, scenes backstage at a theatre, New York streets, and when I was with the ballad singer I did a cover for one of her albums. While I'm here I shall paint local views, local people and, with luck, sell the pictures later.'

'This is why you changed your mind about coming to Mauritius?'

'Yes. I'm here to make money for the future, whereas—' she paused '—you're making the best of the situation.'

Lorcan frowned, but said nothing.

'People have been eager to buy my work,' Jess continued, 'and that's given me the confidence to decide to go freelance and see if I can earn a living from my painting—which is what I shall do when I return home.'

'You're going to pack in being a bodyguard?'

'Yes; the job's taken me around and about and given me some good times, but, like I said, it was never my choice.'

They talked on for a while, about her painting and later about the kind of people she had protected.

'Were you intending to celebrate with the champagne last week?' Lorcan enquired as he finished his whisky.

'No, someone sent me six bottles to the office. I gave the other five away and I was going to give that one away, too.'

'Until you hosed me down,' he said, with the arch of a brow. 'You don't like champagne?'

Her hazel eyes clouded. 'Yes, I do, but I don't like the man who sent it to me.' She rose to her feet. 'I'm tired, so I'll say goodnight.' She looked at the open window. 'Will you close it?'

'Yes, ma'am.'

'The front and back doors are locked, but if you go outside you will be certain to lock up?'

'I will,' Lorcan assured her. 'Goodnight.'

Although Jess fell asleep within minutes, in the early hours of the morning she suddenly came awake. Wide awake. She tossed and turned for what seemed like ages, counted sheep, and when that did not do the trick decided to get herself a drink of water.

Drawing on the short-sleeved shirt, she made her way quietly through to the kitchen. According to a guidebook on Mauritius which she had bought at the airport and read intermittently on the plane, the tap water was not recommended for drinking, so she took a bottle of mineral water from the fridge.

She was filling a glass when the door swung open and Lorcan came into the room.

Her heart missed a beat. She had wondered what he would look like stripped and in just a pair of navy silk boxer shorts he was a beautiful male animal. His skin was golden, his muscles well toned, his chest carried a sprinkling of dark fuzz, while a narrow line arrowed over the flatness of his stomach and down.

'Hello,' she said chokily.

He frowned, his gaze running from her rumpled blonde head, over his shirt and down the length of her long legs to her feet.

'Hi,' he replied.

'Would you—?' She heard herself croak, took a breath and started again. 'Would you like some water?'

'Please.' He walked towards her, his loose-limbed grace and economy of movement sending a silvery tingle through her blood. 'Thanks,' he said as she handed him her glass and reached for another. 'You couldn't sleep?'

'I did for a while, but then I woke up. How about you?' Jess asked, needing to keep on talking.

Something in the way he looked at her was sending jangles through her system. It made her conscious of how she was naked beneath his shirt. The white cotton was fine and she did not need to glance down to guess that the dark aureoles of her nipples would be visible—and maybe even the bushy triangle between her thighs.

Her heart thudded. They were alone together in the middle of the night. A man with raging hormones and a woman who had not made love for what had begun to seem like an excruciatingly long time.

'I haven't slept at all. Earlier you mentioned women being natural observers,' Lorcan said, resting a hip against the kitchen table while he drank the water. 'Is that why you were checking me out in the lift?'

'Of course. It was an awareness exercise,' she declared, trying her best to sound gloriously offhand.

'And what did you like?'

'Like?'

'As the champagne burst you were saying you liked—what?' A grin pulled at the corners of his mouth. 'My noble looks, my raw masculinity, my—'

'Your tie,' she said.

Lorcan sighed noisily. 'And there was I, figuring you were about to proposition me.'

'Proposition?' Jess repeated, with care.

'Suggest we join together for a rapturous liaison.'

'In the lift?'

He nodded. 'OK, even with the stop-go ascent it would've needed to be quick, but—' he slung her an amused look '—who knows, we may've missed out on the most thrilling sixty seconds of our entire lives.'

Jess took a hasty mouthful of water. As she had reacted badly with the exploding magnum, so her reactions now were pathetic. His fantasy of love-making had sent images whirling in her head; her cheeks burned hot, her heart was jackhammering. Having been brought up with three brothers, she prided herself on never being fazed by anything which a member of the opposite sex might do or say—but Lorcan Hunter seemed to be the exception.

Yet the most fazing part was that the images were graphic and lustily appealing. For one crazy moment she had found herself wishing they had shared a liaison, and never mind that they were strangers and it would have occurred with feverish haste amidst a flurry of champagne-soaked clothes.

'If I don't get some sleep, I'm not going to be any use at the site tomorrow,' Lorcan observed as he drank the water.

'About your work,' she said, being stalwartly matter-of-fact. 'I'd like to come with you to see where you go, how you operate and to make some general observations about your security.'

He put down his glass. 'No, thanks.'

'I know you've said you can look after yourself—' her gaze was drawn again to the golden width of his shoulders '—and that's probably true. However, I might be able to suggest some simple precaution which could help or, who knows, even pick up a clue.'

His blue eyes glittered. 'You're guarding Harriet and only Harriet.'

'All right, but the note referred to both of you so surely it—'

'Must you always argue?' Lorcan demanded.

'I am not arguing,' she said. 'I'm suggesting that if I have a quick reconnoitre—'

'And I'm suggesting that you shut up!'

Jess felt the hot smack of anger. She did not know how it had happened, but a flash-fire seemed to have erupted between them and they were fighting like fiends.

'Sorry if I've rattled your cage,' she said acerbically, 'but keep your voice down otherwise you'll wake Harriet.'

'Once Harriet's asleep, a ten-ton truck could drive through her room and she wouldn't wake up,' Lorcan declared, though he lowered his tone into a husky snarl. 'Did anyone ever tell you that you can be an infuriating woman?'

She straightened her shoulders, which thrust out her breasts. 'All the time.'

'How about a sexy one?' he growled, and, hooking a hand around her neck, he yanked her close and kissed her.

His mouth was hard and hot. Taken by surprise, Jess fell against him and discovered that his body was hard and hot, too. His shirt made a thin barrier between them and she could feel the heat of his flesh, the firm chest muscles, was aware of his masculine strength.

Putting her hands on his waist to steady herself, she opened her mouth to protest. It was a mistake, for as her lips parted his plundering tongue slid between them.

Jess's head swam. Sensations streaked through her body—sensations like desire and carnal need. Somewhere amidst the roaring in her brain a voice told her to draw back and, if Lorcan objected, to kick him on the shins, but the sweet roughness of his kiss and the taste of him was sapping her resistance. That's right, girl, she thought, play hard to get.

As if sensing her submission, he released his grip and his hand slid from her neck to caress the peach-bloom skin of her cheek. All anger had gone. His kiss softened and deepened, his tongue grazing against hers in a seductive matching mating rhythm. And as he kissed her his fingers trailed slowly down over her jaw, the column of her throat, to the open neck of the shirt.

Jess spread her hands at his waist. Her breasts were swelling, her nipples distending. He was going to touch her and she wanted him to touch her. She wanted to feel his fingers on the hardening pinnacles . . . and the rasp of his tongue. She wanted—

Lorcan stepped back, breaking all contact. His eyes were heavy-lidded and his breathing was laboured. As the kiss had reduced her to a yearning, quivering mass, so it had had a serious effect on him.

'You will not come to the hotel site,' he said.

She gazed at him. Hotel site? she thought numbly. Oh, the hotel site. 'What—whatever you wish,' she stammered.

'And you will not give me a hundred handy hints on how to foil a kidnapper.'

Attempting a recovery, Jess shrugged. 'You're the boss.'

'And I intend to remain so,' Lorcan said, and turned and strode out of the kitchen.

CHAPTER FOUR

JESS looked beyond the gaggle of arriving children and down the length of the church hall. 'There's just the one entrance?' she enquired.

'That's right. The door to the left of the stage leads into the kitchen and the bathrooms are on the right, but none have access from outside.'

She smiled. This made her job much easier. 'When the weather's fine I shall be somewhere within calling distance outside,' she said, 'but if it rains would you mind if I come and sit quietly indoors?'

'Please do.'

As one of the helpers told Lorcan and Harriet about the morning's activities, Jess was speaking to Madame Floriane who ran the play-school. Keeping her story brief, she had explained that a kidnap threat had been received and, although it could well be a hoax and there was no cause for alarm, she had been retained to ensure Harriet's safety.

Madame Floriane, who was a middle-aged Franco-Mauritian, had replied with a Gallic shrug. She took everything in her stride, including Jess's presence and, it seemed, her somewhat incongruous appearance in a man's shirt and shorts, worn with high black stiletto heels.

'How many children attend the school?' Jess enquired.

'Thirty. They're mostly from expatriate families, though we do have a number of locals. You see the little Chinese girl over there? Her parents own the restaurant in the village and live in the house next door to the one which Monsieur Hunter has rented. I'll tell him, and I'll introduce Harriet to Choo. Perhaps they'll be friends.'

'That would be good,' she said.

As Madame Floriane disappeared, she circumnavigated an obstacle course of a Wendy house, collection of tricycles and numerous running, squealing, toy-toting kids to inspect the kitchen and bathrooms. All had barred windows which ruled out a forced entry.

When she returned to the hall, Harriet was seated beside the little Chinese girl at a play table. Jess felt a pang as sharp as a pain. Choo was chattering energetically to a child on her other side, while Harriet looked very small, very frightened and very alone.

'What did the lady say you're going to do this morning?' she asked, crouching down beside her.

Harriet's big blue eyes filled with tears and she needed to press her lips together before she could answer. 'Make a kite,' she whispered.

'We'll fly it this afternoon, high in the sky,' Jess said enthusiastically, and gave her a hug. A helper appeared armed with sheets of coloured paper and crayons. 'Bye.'

The little girl pressed her lips together again. 'Bye.'

Lorcan was still talking with Madame Floriane, so she walked over to the door to wait.

'You understand that my daughter isn't to be released to anyone apart from Miss Pallister and myself,' she heard him say. 'Not to another woman, even if she should tell you she knows her and claims to be a relative or a friend.'

'I do,' the play-school proprietress assured him.

'It's of vital importance,' he said gravely, and after receiving another assurance crossed back to have another few words with Harriet and take his leave.

Jess frowned. What had prompted him to issue that warning? she wondered. Did he have some particular reason?

'Will you come and collect me when it's home time?' Harriet appealed, keeping her head low and speaking in a watery voice. 'Please, Daddy.'

Lorcan reached down a hand to affectionately stroke her chestnut hair. 'I'll be here, fishface,' he promised.

'Thank you,' she whispered.

'I do hope Harriet's going to be all right,' Jess said, when he joined her and they went outside.

'She will be. She's very adaptable.' A muscle tightened in his jaw. 'The poor kid's had to be.'

Jess drew down the sunglasses which she had pushed onto the top of her head. Yesterday's rain had been replaced by clear blue skies and bright sun, and the light dazzled.

'Harriet was so brave. She wanted to cry, but she wouldn't,' she said, blinking behind the dark lenses.

It was hard not to respond to the little girl, who, when she was in the right mood, was a charmer. If she had burst into tears she would have understood and felt sorry, yet her courage had been even more touching.

Lorcan looked at her. 'And now you want to cry? Beneath the toughie exterior hides a big soft heart.'

'Mine isn't the only one,' she protested. 'You agreed to break off from work and come for her at lunchtime.'

He smiled and suddenly there was a bond between them. 'Yes, but it is her first day.'

'You said you'd ring the airport and ask if there's any news about my luggage,' Jess reminded him as he opened the door of the Jeep and climbed inside.

She had intended to telephone before they left the bungalow, but there had not been time. The arrival of Naseem, a dumpy, softly spoken Indian woman of around her own age, had slowed everything down. It was probably because she wanted to make a good impression, but the housekeeper had been so precise about setting the table and preparing toast and coffee that breakfast had taken far longer than anticipated and, in the end, they had had to rush out with minutes to spare.

'Will do,' Lorcan assured her.

When would her cases arrive? Jess wondered as the four-wheel drive disappeared along the quiet road. The most likely theory seemed to be that they had been offloaded by mistake in the Seychelles and could appear today. So she had decided to postpone the purchase of any clothes until tomorrow.

Turning, she undertook a survey of her surroundings. The hall was a quaint black and white building with a dark pink corrugated-iron roof. To its right stood the church, which was a similar, though larger, construction with a pink corrugated, white-capped bell tower. On the left of the hall, a lawn sloped down to a sandy track edged by orange-blossomed flamboyant trees and beyond the track lay the harbour.

Her gaze stretched. The two fishing smacks which were tied up beside the stone jetty indicated that it was a working harbour, but all the other craft which bobbed at moorings on the sun-spangled and amaz-ingly turquoise water were for pleasure. She noted a glass-bottomed boat, several pristine white cabin cruisers, sailing dinghies and a handful of speed-boats. On the far side of the harbour, a small wooden hut advertised 'boats for hire', while beside it was parked a mobile food wagon which sold peeled pine-apples, water melon and soft drinks.

Needing to step carefully in her high heels, Jess walked across the lawn to the shade of the trees. She sat down. This would be the perfect place from which to monitor who came and went at the play-school—and to paint. She had a good view of the life of the harbour and, if she turned her head, could see the deeper blue of the ocean beyond and lavender shapes of distant offshore islands. As she absorbed the colours, the clarity of light, the tranquillity, Jess smiled. Her job had taken her to different lands and exciting places, but she had never been anywhere which was so close to paradise.

Last night when Lorcan had kissed her, she had been close to paradise. Her smile faded. For a few foolish moments. But his kiss had been contrarily in-spired by the heat of anger and had been swiftly re-gretted. He would have been cursing himself when he returned to bed.

She had wondered if he might make some caustic dismissive comment about the tempestuous embrace this morning, but he had ignored it. She wished she could. But the touch of his lips had been the first thing she had thought about on waking and she was reliving their pressure again now.

Taking off her sunglasses, Jess chewed fractiously at the end of a side-bar. Why, when some kisses left

her cold—like Roscoe Dunbar's—had she responded
with such enthusiasm last night? Jet lag was a feeble
excuse. It could only be due to that much flaunted
and slightly mythical idea—chemistry. And Lorcan's
trailing fingers had indicated that he had fallen victim
to it, too. Briefly. She snapped the sunglasses closed.
A chemical reaction between them was something she
could do without.

Opening the guidebook which she had brought
along, she turned to the introduction. One kiss would
not be allowed to tie her up in knots. She was made
of sterner stuff. Her gaze fixed on the page. She had
decided to spend today settling into her surroundings
and learning more about Mauritius, and leave any
thoughts of painting until tomorrow.

With one eye on the hall—and one tense ear because it seemed possible that Harriet might eventually
succumb to tears, at which point she would rush
inside—Jess started to read. Halfway through the
morning she bought herself a cool drink, and settled
beneath the flamboyant trees again. She was deep into
the colourful history of the island, which after being
a bolt-hole for pirates and corsairs had been colon-
ised by first the French and later by the British, when
she heard the thrum of a car engine. She glanced up.
The Jeep Cherokee was approaching. But the play-
school did not finish for another twenty minutes.

As the vehicle swung in off the road, Jess rose,
brushed blades of grass from her backside and set off
precariously up the lawn. She had reached the edge
of the gravelled parking ground when Lorcan killed
the engine and vaulted out. Her heart seemed to hit
her throat. Wearing a yellow hard hat and in khaki
shirt and blue jeans worn white at stress points, he

was the working man—all sinew, all muscle, all capable strength. For someone who had spent half the night awake he looked in marvellously good health.

'You're early,' she called.

'I wanted to be on time. You haven't heard anguished sobs all morning?'

His question was jokey, but the concern she heard in his voice indicated that he, too, had spent much of the past three hours worrying about Harriet. Whatever his other faults, she had to admit that when it came to being a parent his heart was in the right place.

'None,' she said, walking up. 'So the doting daddy needn't have— Yeeow!'

One of her needle-thin heels had skidded on a larger stone hidden amidst the gravel and, suddenly, her arms were windmilling, her book and shoulderbag went flying, she was stumbling, tripping, falling. Falling forwards. Falling against Lorcan.

'Oh!' Jess gasped as she slammed into him.

He absorbed the impact, his arms going around her and keeping her upright. He held her firm. 'You can never resist the dramatic moment, can you?' he enquired, his tone a mixture of humour and irritation.

In her heels she was almost his height and as she looked into his eyes something fluttered inside her. She saw desire in their blue depths. A desire which created an immediate answering desire within her. Damn, damn, damn. That traitorous, treacherous chemistry was working again. And it annoyed him as much as it unsettled her.

Jess drummed up a smile. 'Sorry. Accident-prone.'

'But only with me.'

Her pulses throbbed. Held in the circle of his arms, her only awareness was of him. Of the smouldering blue eyes, his body against hers, of the unconscious huskiness of his voice.

She stepped back, making him release her. Physical attraction might be a powerful force, but she refused to go gaga over a man who, at best, was putting up with her.

'Only with you. A strange phenomenon,' she said, trying to sound flip.

Lorcan bent to retrieve her book and her bag. 'No sobs, but how about suspicious characters?' he asked as he handed them to her.

'Not seen any,' Jess replied, thinking that if a platoon of suspicious characters had marched past with trumpets blaring a moment ago she would not have noticed them. Nether had she noticed the arrival of a couple of cars behind them nor the mothers with pushchairs who were starting to assemble outside the hall. She cast him a frowning look. 'I heard you talking to Madame Floriane about a female kidnapper.'

'It's possible,' he said, before she could get any further.

'I'm aware of that. I have thought around the matter.' Her chin lifted. 'I am a professional.'

'So you keep saying. Ad infinitum.'

She razored a smile. 'Only because it's true and you seem a little slow on the uptake. However, I wondered why you—'

'If a stranger snatched Harriet the alarm would be raised immediately, but if they reckoned to have some kind of association and offered a plausible excuse for taking her away then two or three hours might go by before it was realised that she'd been abducted. And, to quote you, it pays to be sensible. I spoke to the airport,' Lorcan went on, without a pause, 'and they've located your luggage.'

'Oh . . . great,' she said, taking the necessary mental leap and smiling. 'Where is it?'

'In Delhi.'

'Delhi?' Jess repeated, in wide-eyed disbelief.

'Seems there was a flight leaving for there around the same time as ours and your cases were loaded onto the wrong plane. But they're being returned to Gatwick and sent on here, which the guy reckoned should take another couple of days.' Removing the hard hat, he riffled a hand through his hair. 'So if you want to buy clothes I'll run you round to the shops as soon as Harriet appears.'

She sighed. 'Yes, please.'

As with lending her his clothes, Lorcan's offer was generous, for on this, his first day back at work, he must be under pressure. Their thrown-together relationship was riven with contradictions, Jess thought as they waited. One minute they were involved in a battle of wills, the next everything was friendly. She looked at him from beneath the thick fringe of her lashes. And although she might be an unwelcome guest in his household he lusted after her. It was a conflict to wrestle with, she thought drily.

'Here's Harriet,' Lorcan said, and she turned to see that the double doors of the hall had been opened and children were pouring out.

Jess smiled with relief. The little girl who had emerged into the sunshine was relaxed and happy. She was too busy chattering to Choo and a little boy to see them at first, but when she did she skipped merrily over.

'You were right, it was fun,' Harriet told her, and brandished a lime-green kite with a haphazardly tied butterfly tail. 'Marion—she's one of the helpers—said my kite was *très bien*. That means very good. It's French. They speak French in France,' she informed them, in that solemn way of four-year-olds. 'After we made our kites, me and Choo played in the Wendy house and I learned some writing—'

'French writing?' Lorcan enquired.

She giggled. 'No, silly. Proper writing. And—'

As they climbed into the four-wheel drive and drove through the village, Harriet treated them to a non-stop commentary on her morning. She was still talking when Lorcan halted outside the row of shops. And as they made their way along.

'This is the only one which sells clothes,' Jess said, looking in through the open door of a gift shop. She grimaced at a display of gaudy T-shirts which fought for space amongst replicas of old sailing ships, patchwork Creole dolls, embroidered tablecloths and postcard stands. 'But they don't specialise in high fashion.'

'Port Louis, the capital, has plenty of decent stores,' Lorcan said, 'but it's around thirty miles away and right now it's impossible for me to take that much time off work. You could go by taxi or bus, or hire a car—'

'I only need to manage for a couple of days so I'll make do with things from here,' she decided, and they went inside.

The shop was empty and the effusive greeting of the girl who came to serve them suggested they could easily be the first customers of the day. As Lorcan and Harriet went to look at a display of china animals, Jess explained how her luggage had been temporarily mislaid and that she required sandals, a T-shirt and shorts, and a swimsuit.

Rushing around and determined to please, the girl produced what seemed to be her entire stock. The only sandals available in her size were thick-soled rubber flip-flops, but Jess took them. She also settled for a T-shirt and shorts set in hectic rainbow colours. When it came to a bathing costume, she hesitated. Whilst it would be bliss to swim, did she want to do so clad in an aggressively boned contraption which was patterned with purple roses?

'You try,' the girl insisted, ushering her into the makeshift curtained cubicle which was erected in one corner. 'I find more.'

Jess had shed her shirt and shorts when the curtain was ripped aside.

'How about this?' the girl enquired, holding up a bikini in a hideous maroon seersucker.

Conscious of standing there in her bra and panties, she shook her head. She might wear not much more on a beach, yet to be suddenly revealed with a rattle of curtain rings and a swish made her feel like a peepshow. Although Lorcan was talking to Harriet as they inspected the pottery, his glance had flicked her way. She could not blame him. If their situations had been reversed, she felt sure her eyes would have been drawn to him.

'No, thanks, I'll stick with the one-piece,' she said hastily.

The assistant went away and during her absence she made a rapid change from underwear to swimsuit.

She was only just in time for seconds later the girl reappeared, casually wafting back the curtain. She appeared to believe that Lorcan was her husband, Harriet her child and so rated any nudity as insignificant.

'Come and show,' she ordered, taking hold of her wrist, and before Jess could protest she found herself being yanked without ceremony out into the aisle. 'Pretty?' the girl demanded.

Turning, Lorcan took one long, all-encompassing look. 'Delectable,' he murmured, his gaze fixing on Jess's breasts.

Again, she could not blame him. Although she was slim, the breasts which sprang from her narrow ribcage were surprisingly curvy and, pushed up by the tight boned bodice, seemed in imminent danger of spilling out.

'Too small,' she declared, needing to fight the urge to shield herself from his gaze with crossed hands.

'You think so?' His mouth quirked. 'I don't. I'd say well-nigh perfection.'

Jess gritted her teeth. When he lost his temper she could cope, but let him make a sexual reference and her poise shattered. She had never had any patience with females who took a fit of the vapours in the presence of an attractive male, but she seemed to be acting in a similar way herself. It was inexplicable, infantile and maddening.

'What about this costume?' the assistant suggested, indicating a sleek black cut-away number which was pinned to the wall behind the counter and which she had not noticed.

Summoning up her bravado, she stalked past Lorcan to take a look. 'It's closer to the kind of thing which I had in mind,' she said, and inspected the price tag. 'But it'd put me over the allowance and I don't want to spend any more.'

'I'll buy it for you,' he offered.

'No, thanks.'

'No?' he protested, sounding surprised.

'I prefer to pay my own way. I'll pass on a swimsuit, but take the other things,' she told the girl, and returned to the cubicle.

This time, she managed to get back into her clothes without any interruption.

Naseem's precision on her first day had been a warning of things to come, Jess thought wearily two afternoons later. Whatever the task, be it brushing the veranda or dusting or washing up, the housekeeper did it thoroughly, but she was so *slow*. She had been ironing for over an hour, and whilst every garment she had done would have won gold medals for flawless pressing half the pile of dried washing continued to languish on the kitchen table.

'Mr Hunter will be home soon,' Jess said, 'so shall I prepare the vegetables for dinner?'

'Mmm,' Naseem replied dreamily.

A gentle character who wore floating saris, she spent most of the day in a dream and her thoroughness had a sleep-walking quality about it. She had proudly revealed that next year she was to be married to 'a lawyer with his own practice', so presumably the daydreams were about him.

As Jess was peeling potatoes, Harriet wandered in. After an afternoon playing on the beach with Choo, the little girl was pink-cheeked and tousled. Sitting down at the table, she opened her haversack, which she continually hauled around, and brought out a bundle of photographs.

'This is my mummy,' she said, flourishing a well-thumbed snap in front of the housekeeper.

The unhurried ironing did not falter. 'Mmm,' Naseem said.

'She was called Sara and she was American.'

'Mmm.'

Dissatisfied with the tepid response, Harriet swivelled in her chair. 'This is a picture of my mummy,' she said, holding the coloured photograph out towards Jess.

As she bent forward to take a look, a claw of jealousy scratched inside her. She had thought that Lorcan's wife would be beautiful and she was. She had pansy-size dark eyes set in an oval face, classically refined features and a waterfall of long brown hair which swirled around her shoulders. Heroine's hair. A great romantic heroine. A twentieth-century Scarlett O'Hara.

Recognising that she had captured an interested audience, Harriet delved into the bundle again. 'And this is my daddy with my mummy.'

In a full-length snap, Lorcan was standing with his arm around his wife in a sunlit garden. They were smiling.

'They look very happy,' Jess observed, and resumed her potato-peeling.

Sara Hunter had been petite. A fragile, ultra-feminine creature who must have inspired macho cherishing emotions in her husband, she thought, suddenly feeling as overgrown and gangly as she had done at school. The woman could never have been a bodyguard. The idea was absurd. She had needed protection from the slings and arrows of the world and oodles of tender loving care.

'My mummy and daddy used to take me on picnics in California,' Harriet declared, 'and they bought me great big ice-creams.'

'Your daddy told you that?' she said.

'No, I remember.' The little girl thrust out her chin as if to deflect an objection. 'I can remember my mummy tucking me up in bed and singing songs to me and cuddling me when I had a bad dream. I can remember everything, even when I was a baby. One day my mummy and my daddy and me went to—'

As she launched into a long and garbled story about a picnic beside a lake, Jess sighed. Harriet had only been two when her mother had died, so these were not true memories. She must be repeating what Lorcan and other people had told her, or she was making it up. She sensed it was probably the latter. Yet whether her memories were second-hand or imaginary they were necessary. Talking about her mother comforted her and kept her image alive, which would help fill the gap the little girl must feel when she saw other children with their mummies.

Jess had prepared the potatoes, snow peas and sweetcorn which were to accompany the roast chicken which Naseem had—thankfully— already put in the oven, when the doorbell rang.

'It's my daddy,' Harriet declared, putting the photographs back into her haversack and clambering down.

'I don't think so,' she said as she followed her out into the hall. 'He has a key. Perhaps it's Flat Stanley?' she suggested, referring to a character in one of the

books which Lorcan had read to his daughter on
the plane.

Harriet's blue eyes danced. 'Or Batman?' she said,
joining in the game. 'Or Mr Blobby or—?'

Jess opened the door. 'Even better,' she said,
grinning at the airline employee who stood there, 'it's
my luggage.'

Being reunited with the belongings which she had
begun to wonder if she would ever see again made
her feel as if it was her birthday and Christmas rolled
into one. With Harriet watching and enthusiastically
helping, she unpacked. Dresses were hung in the
wardrobe, her underwear placed in drawers—there
need be no more nightly rinsing through of bra and
panties—paperbacks were arranged on shelves in the
living room.

Changing into new clothes from the skin out, she
carried the cast-offs through to the kitchen and slung
them into the washing machine.

'These are for washing tomorrow,' she told Naseem,
who had finally completed the ironing and was setting
the table.

The housekeeper nodded. 'Mmm. You look good,'
she added, in an unusual show of interest.

Jess smiled. She was wearing a sleeveless coral
ribbed top with a gently scooped neckline and
parchment-coloured tailored trousers. They were her
own clothes which had a degree of style and
which *fitted*.

'Real good,' a deeper voice said, and Lorcan walked
into the room.

'Thank you, kind sir,' she replied.

As he picked up Harriet and listened to her chatter,
his eyes remained on Jess. She grinned. His look was

jangling through her system again, but she did not care. She wanted to bask in his admiration—even if it was destined to be short-lived.

'Have you had a hard day?' she asked, for there was a mesh of fine lines around his eyes and he looked tired.

He nodded. 'I've been continually on the go and it's so damned hot.'

'Cooler tomorrow,' Naseem declared, and collected her bag. She waddled to the door. 'See you in the morning.'

'You don't need to bath me tonight, Daddy,' Harriet said, when the housekeeper had departed. 'Jess can do it.'

Lorcan shook his head. 'That isn't one of Jess's duties.'

'It's OK,' she said. 'I'll bath Harriet, just this once.'

'You look a trifle damp,' Lorcan remarked, when she walked out onto the wide back veranda a couple of hours later. He grinned. 'Harriet didn't have a bottle of champagne in the bath?'

'No, but she thought it was great fun to flick her fingers.' Jess glanced down at her splashed coral top. 'It'll soon dry, and the next time I supervise I shall make sure that I stand well back.'

'The next time?'

'You work a long day and—well, it was fun.'

He nodded towards his glass of whisky which sat on the low table beside him. 'Want one?'

He was sprawled in a curvaceous wicker chair with his long legs stretched out. Before dinner, he had showered and changed into a dusky pink sports shirt and dark trousers. His blue-black hair tumbled over his brow and he was barefoot. Her heart missed a beat. A panther at rest.

'No, thanks, I'll stick with this,' she replied, rattling the ice in the tumbler of sparkling water which she had brought out with her.

Jess sat down. The sun had almost set and beyond the garden the fields which sloped gently up into the foothills of the mountains were gilded a deep gold. The evening was still and the air balmy. The only sound was the occasional whirr of wings as a brilliant-hued dragon fly helicoptered by.

'Did you speak to your brother this afternoon?' Lorcan enquired.

'Yes, though there wasn't anything to report.' For a moment, she wondered whether she should quiz him again about Charles Sohan and the reality of the hotelier making a threat, but decided to leave it for now. He would be irked by her quizzing and she was reluctant to disrupt this peaceful time of day. 'How's the hotel progressing?'

'It's going great. Knock on wood,' he said, rapping his knuckles on the table. 'The two guys I left in charge while I went home kept up the pressure, and now all the major building work is done and we're a week ahead of schedule.'

'The men are from your own company?'

Lorcan nodded. 'I have a staff of six, working out of an office near my home. The guys who're here are both single and heavily into diving and water sports, so whenever they get a spare minute it's on with the masks and out to the coral reefs. Or off for a spot of deep-sea fishing.'

'Sir Peter spoke of the development as a hotel village,' Jess recalled. 'What does that mean?'

He sat forward, his tiredness falling away as enthusiasm took over. 'It means there's a central multilevelled and open-plan building which includes the reception area, offices, bar and two restaurants which look onto what'll be the largest fresh-water swimming pool on the island, while the guest accommodation is in individual thatched cottages. The cottages will be set amidst landscaped gardens, enjoying complete privacy and all with ocean views. We're catering for the seriously rich here.'

'So the cottages are to be luxurious?'

'The last word,' he said, and told her how they would have Yorkstone floors, built-in furniture crafted from Brazilian woods and marble Jacuzzis.

She smiled. 'Dreams are made of this.'

'That's part of the job, realising people's dreams.'

'When did you decide you wanted to be an architect?'

'When I was six.'

Her brows rose. 'That young?'

'My father had his own building firm and when I was a kid he used to take me with him to houses which he was constructing. That gave me the initial interest.' Lorcan grinned, sampling his whisky. 'Though I thought being an architect would be glamorous, whereas most of it's the usual daily grind.'

'Have you always worked on hotels?' Jess asked.

'No, I've designed and overseen the construction of a number of private dwellings, but hotels are my speciality. My first job with Dowling's was restoring Victorian pubs for a major brewing company and when they sent me to the States I renovated a couple of twenties-era hotels in New York,' he explained. 'After I left them I reverted to homes for a while, but then I won a contract for a green-field-site hotel outside Dallas, followed on with one in Barbados, and last year I built a hotel development in the South of France.'

'And now you're building one here. You've moved around.'

'Yes, but as from next year when Harriet starts school I shall only accept work which is within driving distance of home.'

'That'll restrict your career.'

'Drastically, but it can't be helped. She's been shuffled around enough in her short life and she needs stability. It'd be different if she had a mother to provide a continuous presence,' he said, and frowned. 'But my parents are getting on in years and it's unfair to expect them to take charge when I go away. Besides which they spoil her silly, so she always needs knocking back into shape when I return. And Harriet hates being left with nannies.'

'How many nannies have you had?' she enquired.

'Four. Senga and three girls back in the States. They were pleasant enough and efficient, but they all had serious boyfriends which seemed to mean they always had other, more important things on their minds.'

'Like Naseem does?'

He seemed surprised by the observation. 'I guess.'

'This afternoon Harriet was showing her photographs of you and your wife, presumably in California?'

Lorcan sat back. 'It would be. That's where Sara was from and where we lived.'

'She was beautiful.'

He gazed out across the fields to the mountain. The last rays of the sun had disappeared and the land was shadowy, stepped in twilight. 'Yes.'

'And young to die.'

'She was thirty,' he said, his voice clipped. He took a slug of whisky. 'The guy who gave you the champagne. Was he someone whom you'd guarded?'

Jess looked at him. She had wondered whether, like Harriet, he might want to talk about his wife and find it a solace, but the beautiful Mrs Hunter was clearly a no-go area. And by terminating the conversation Lorcan had issued a warning to her to keep off.

'Yes, it was Roscoe Dunbar, the actor.'

He raised his brows. 'The thinking woman's heart-throb.'

'If the blond, suave, raffish type appeals.'

'Someone had threatened him?'

She shook her head. 'He was off on a country-wide tour with a play and he persuaded the management to hire a female bodyguard because it made him seem different and more important.'

'Hang on,' Lorcan said suddenly. 'About six months ago, didn't I read something about him being cornered by a fan who believed he'd slighted her and intended to stab him, but he was rescued by a girl? Rescued by you?'

'It was me, but the newspapers dramatised the event beyond all recognition. The woman was a nutcase and whilst she did have a penknife in her bag she made no attempt to use it. She just threw herself onto him and I pulled her off. Anyone could've done it.'

He slid a hand into the neck of his sports shirt, idly rubbing at the whorls of dark hair. 'But I read about how full of gratitude the guy was.'

'Roscoe was grateful because he's a coward and, for a moment, he believed there was a danger he might get hurt. But his gratitude also made great publicity, which he loves. He has an ego the size of a house.'

'Which is why you don't like him?'

'One reason, though my main objection is his willingness to cheat on his wife, despite being "gloriously happily married with two magnificent children"—as he always claims.'

'He wanted to cheat on her with you?'

'He did. The tour had only just started when the fan leapt on him, so when he showed an interest in me—as in forever hugging me—I assumed it was simply because he was grateful, and an actor. I didn't take it seriously.' She paused, distracted by Lorcan's massaging and wondering what the rasp of hair would feel like beneath *her* fingers. She sat straighter. 'Then one evening Roscoe insisted he needed to speak to me in private. I agreed to go to his hotel room where he kissed me, tried to separate me from my clothes and force me into bed.'

'Tried?'

'The application of a knee to a sensitive part of his anatomy enabled me to make a get-away.'

He laughed. 'And left him writhing?'

'With tears in his eyes. I thought I'd made it painfully obvious that I failed to find him attractive, but his ego didn't seem able to accept it and he continued to sidle close. Even though we were in public and sometimes his wife was around.'

'A guy who liked to live dangerously,' he remarked.

'I'm afraid so. The tour ended and for almost three months I heard nothing. I was sure I'd escaped when, out of the blue, Roscoe sent me the champagne with a loving message. To the Citadel office because I've kept my home address a secret.' She shuddered. 'I don't want him turning up there. My first reaction was to send the crate straight back, but it would've cost and I thought he might simply have it delivered back to me again. So I decided to give the champagne away, then—'

'Who was going to have my bottle?' Lorcan interrupted.

'The old lady who lives in the flat below me. Then I thought I'd ring and explain what I'd done, and tell him his gifts were not welcome,' she continued. 'I did, but he took no notice. Instead he vowed that he cared for me and said his wife had got fed up with his ''peccadilloes'', as he called it, and was planning to leave him.'

'So it was the green light for the two of you?'

Jess sighed. 'That was how he saw it, but it frightened me. His wife was suspicious before and if he continues to show an interest she might decide to quote my name, with the others, in their divorce. If there was a man around Roscoe'd leave me alone, but unfortunately he knows I'm on my own.'

'You couldn't claim to still be involved with the guy you were almost engaged to?' Lorcan suggested.

'No. That was a couple of years ago and now he's happily married to someone else.'

'You don't mind?'

She shook her head. 'At the time I believed it was true love, but, in retrospect, I think it was his image I fell for rather than him. Mark was a model for a book-jacket hero.'

'Mr Clean-Cut?'

She grinned. 'Tom Cruise, eat your heart out.'

'You lived together?'

'Yes, but I was often away on assignments and it didn't take long before our relationship ran out of steam. We weren't compatible. For instance, I can get ready to go out in half an hour max, but it used to take him ages. He'd blow-dry his hair and agonise over what to wear, and when we finally made it he was forever looking at himself in mirrors.' She grimaced. 'I think I was something of a disappointment, because I didn't admire him enough.'

'You're going to be out of the country for the next three months, so perhaps Roscoe Dunbar will forget about admiring you,' Lorcan said.

She nodded. 'That's what I'm hoping.'

She had never been properly in love, Jess reflected as she lay in bed that night. She had had her fair share of boyfriends, but, apart from Mark, they had not been serious. And because she did not believe in one-night stands her sexual history was sparse. Yet sex was an integral part of life and she was beginning to feel as if she might be missing out.

A thought popped into her head. When they had come in from the veranda and said goodnight, Lorcan had locked the kitchen door. But had he shot the bolts? She switched on the bedside lamp. She had no sense of immediate danger from kidnappers—or, frankly, of *any* danger—yet security was the name of the game.

Climbing out of bed, she pulled on an over-sized boat-necked T-shirt which she used as a stand-by nightgown and tiptoed forward. She had almost reached the door when something scuttled across the floorboards an inch or so in front of her toes. Jess gazed down in horror. It was a cockroach.

'No!' she squeaked as the intruder abruptly stopped as if contemplating a change of direction and an assault on *her*. Her skin crawled. She went cold. The insect was black and shiny, with twitchy antennae sticking out of its head. 'No!' she yelped, frozen to the spot when it started to move in an erratic zig-zag past her.

'Is something the matter?' Lorcan asked, outside in the hall.

With one leap, she was at the door and flinging it open. 'It's—it's a cockroach,' she jabbered, frantically pointing. 'It's enormous. See it, there! Get rid of it! Now! Please!'

He took a couple of steps inside and laughed. 'It's just a little ol' bug.'

'Little?' Jess protested, staring at the still trekking scuttler. She dared not let it disappear from sight. If it disappeared, she would lie awake all night wondering where it had gone and if it might suddenly decide to trek over her. She shivered. Then she would *die*!

'Got a newspaper?' Lorcan enquired.

'A magazine,' she said, grabbing for a copy of *Vanity Fair* which lay on the bedside table. The cockroach changed direction and, with another leap, she was on the bed and drawing up her legs. 'It's coming back!'

He opened the window, scooped up the cockroach and tossed it outside.

'Thank you, thank you,' she babbled, in feverish relief.

'Any time.'

Jess looked across at him in horror. 'You don't mean there could be more?'

'We are in the Tropics,' Lorcan said, closing the window.

'How come you were in the hall?' she asked suddenly.

'I'd been checking that I'd bolted the back door. What were you doing up?'

'I was going to check it, too.'

His eyes gleamed. 'Then you saw a little ol' cockroach. But a cockroach won't hurt you, so there's no need for the hysterical screaming the next time.'

'I did not scream hysterically.'

He sat down on the bed beside her. 'All those shrieks? Sounded like pure hysteria to me. Which just goes to show that, whilst you may be a dab hand with a headlock, when it comes to facing one of the tiniest of God's creatures you still need to call for a man.'

Jess slitted her eyes at him. 'Kiss my ass.'

'Is that an invitation?'

'It's a figure of speech,' she said hastily as it hit her that she was wearing only the baggy T-shirt with nothing underneath, while he wore his trousers but was bare-chested.

'Very eloquent. Though it has crossed my mind.' Lorcan bent his head. 'But suppose I settle for this?'

As she had leapt so frantically onto the bed, the T-shirt had slipped down to reveal the round of one shoulder and he pressed his lips to the warm skin. Her heart jackknifed. She knew she should move and move fast, yet the caress of his mouth seemed to have paralysed her.

'Is this what you wear in bed?' he asked, his gaze dropping to the T-shirt with its well-washed Bugs Bunny motif.

'You think I'm more the—the pink frilly nightie and fluffy mules type?'

Jess was trying to joke, but the air seemed to have thickened in her throat and the words emerged jerkily.

'I think you're the type who sleeps naked,' Lorcan said, and brushed his lips across her shoulder again. 'Right?'

'Right,' she said, on a gulp.

Raising his head, he grinned. 'And the type who goes into a flat spin at the sight of a cockroach.'

His comment shifted them onto firmer ground and she was able to grin back. 'Don't you just love to feel superior?'

'Are you saying that I'm not?'

'I am, and I'm saying that I did not, repeat not—' she pushed her hand against his chest in unthinking emphasis '—go into a flat spin.'

'Did, too.'

She pushed harder. 'Did not!'

'And screamed hysterically.'

'Never!' Jess declared, and pushed again.

This time Lorcan fell back onto the pillow and pulled her down with him. He wrapped an arm around her.

'You're arguing again,' he said, and he kissed her.

His mouth was seeking, yet tender. There was no anger this time. She felt the firm pressure of his lips and the moistness of his tongue against hers. She tasted him. Tasted a faint minty tang of toothpaste and the erotic, wholly personal flavour of him. Eyes closed, Jess abandoned any notion of protest. She wanted to protest against his mouth on hers, his arms around her, the darts of excitement which had begun to prick at her breasts and her groin? No, no and no.

As the kiss moved into another, and another, his large hand stroked down her. Over the swelling curves of her breasts, over the flatness of her stomach to the juncture of her thighs.

'I want to look at you,' Lorcan said softly, and his fingers curled around the hem of her T-shirt. He drew up the soft white cotton and she moved, making it easier for him to pull it off over her head. As he gazed at her, he drew in a ragged breath. 'All smooth, silken woman,' he murmured.

His hand stroked over her again, feeling, caressing, tantalising. Jess arched her back. His thumbs were skimming over the peaks of her breasts, round and around, in a wonderful relentless rhythm. The pricking of excitement was becoming an ache. She stirred restlessly. She needed more.

Seeming to respond to her unspoken plea, he lowered his head and she felt the rasp of his tongue as he savoured her flesh. She moaned low in her throat. Now his teeth were on her nipples, softly biting. Her head reeled. Heat infused her. She wrapped an arm around his neck, her fingers pushing into the thick dark hair at his nape. She had not known that desire could be so greedy, so instant, so strong.

She wanted to touch him and when he drew back to gaze down at her breasts with their glistening points she lifted a hand. Jess stroked his chest, absorbing the texture of his skin, feeling the scour of dark hair, trailing her fingertips across his nipples. As she bent to kiss the flat brown discs, Lorcan stiffened and drew back.

'What's wrong?' she asked.

He placed his hands at her waist as if he needed to control their movements, needed to control himself. 'We must stop.'

'Stop?'

Jess felt the ache of her body and listened to the screaming of her heart. They could not stop now.

Lorcan took a breath. 'I have no protection.'

'Don't worry,' she said, the relief rushing through her. 'I'm on the Pill.'

He rolled away, swinging his feet to the floor and standing upright. 'I prefer to take my own precautions.'

Slowly, she sat up. A moment ago he had been the ardent lover, but not now. As he had changed his mind about recruiting her and about kissing her, so he had changed his mind about making love. Her frustration transformed itself into anger, which started to seethe inside her. How dared he swing hot and cold? How dared he reject her?

Reaching for her T-shirt, Jess dragged it on over her head. 'You think I sleep around?' she demanded, glaring at him. 'You're afraid you might catch some anti-social disease?'

'God, no!'

She frowned. His protest had been harsh—and sounded sincere. 'Then I don't understand. Unless— You think I'm lying about taking the Pill,' she declared. 'You think I'm so damned keen to sleep with you that I'd take chances and to hell with the consequences!'

'I just don't want us to be sucked into something by our hormones,' he said heavily. 'Something which we might both regret.'

'Baloney,' she retorted. 'You don't trust me! Yes, I wanted to sleep with you, like you wanted to sleep with me, but not now. Now I want you to get out of my room—' she jabbed a furious finger at the door '—and stay out!'

Lorcan frowned, pushing his hands into his trouser pockets. He seemed about to speak—to apologise? To protest?—but then he turned on his heel. A moment later, the door clicked shut behind him.

CHAPTER FIVE

JESS studied the two little girls who were playing beneath the shade of a tree in the back garden, then lowered her gaze to the sketch on her pad. For a spur-of-the-moment pencil doodle, it had potential. The curving branch which framed the top of the picture gave a sense of depth, the children in the paddling pool were in proportion, their gleeful smiles looked real. The scene was schmaltzier than those she usually chose to depict, yet it also had charm.

'Now I've made three and you've made three,' Choo declared, counting the mud pies which were arranged on the grass on either side of the blue plastic pool.

'Let's both make four,' Harriet said.

'Let's!' her friend carolled, and they scampered across the lawn, two frolicsome imps in their swimsuits and wavy-brimmed sunhats.

There was some vigorous digging in the loamy soil, buckets were almost filled and toted solemnly back to the pool, water was added.

'Jess, watch us stir,' called Harriet as small hands were plunged in.

'I'm watching,' she assured her.

Maybe it was because Naseem's slow-motion housekeeping left little time for childminding, but over the month spent in Mauritius she had gradually taken on an active childcare role, including regular bathtimes. Whilst this was contrary to her intention, she had no grumbles. It meant that she and her charge had established a rapport, which the little girl enjoyed and which gave her a warm feeling of satisfaction. She had never been particularly conscious of having a maternalistic instinct before, Jess thought wryly, but it seemed to be alive and well and living in the Tropics.

Of course, things were not perpetual sweetness and light. As all children do, Harriet acted up and had her prima donna moments. Like times when she was tired and refused to eat her meals, or asked for a drink only to announce that she did not like it, or when she trampolined on her bed when she was supposed to be getting ready to go out. Then she would scold her, the little girl would sulk, but five minutes later they were friends again.

Jess tugged at the strapless top of her topaz satin bikini. If only her relationship with Lorcan were as straightforward. But it racketed around from the businesslike to the formally polite to occasions when they would talk, engrossed, for hours. She liked to hear his daily report on how the hotel complex was advancing and about past projects, while her body-guarding assignments intrigued him. They also discussed what was happening in the world, books, films et cetera. Yet always she felt a tension. A sexual tension.

As instructed, he had stayed out of her bedroom. And since that evening a month ago he had not touched her nor made any even faintly provocative remark. Their thwarted lovemaking had been studiously ignored, by both of them. But she could not ignore him as a strong, physical and desirable male.

Jess sketched in leaves on the overhead branch. She was always aware of Lorcan. Tinglingly aware. Whenever he walked into the room, her eyes were drawn to the grace of his stride, to the sheen of his bronzed, arms, to how his hair curled thick and dark around his ears. Whenever he came near, the breath seemed to clog in her throat. And on a couple of trips to the beach when he had worn white stretch swim trunks which had left his masculinity in no possible doubt she had damn near hyperventilated!

She scowled. Her fascination with the man was pitiable and the only consolation—if it could be called consolation—was that it worked two ways. She unsettled him as much as he unsettled her. The chemistry persisted. In unguarded moments his blue eyes would flicker hungrily down her body, he became restless, and he was so determined to avoid any contact—as if one brush of his fingers against hers might ignite his passions and send them spinning wildly out of control—that it was almost comical.

Almost. The reason for his restlessness eliminated any humour. Lorcan had wanted to make love, but had not trusted her. She blackened the line around the edge of the paddling pool. His distrust angered and offended her. It cut deep.

This far at the weekends she had used her free time to explore and exercise—taking a bus into Port Louis, running along the shore, sneaking a look at the hotel site which stood on a promontory amidst palm trees and promised to be stylish. But perhaps next weekend she should pack a bag and take off on her own? There were numerous hotels on the island and a couple of days away would allow her—would allow them both—to calm down and cool down. To chill out. The lovemaking that never was could be consigned to history and she would attempt to forget, though she could not forgive, what amounted to his accusation of fraud. Then they would start again, on a far less strenuous, entirely platonic footing.

Where should she go? Jess wondered. Somewhere in the north such as Grande Baie, which was a flourishing holiday resort, or to one of the plateau towns, like Quatre Bornes or Curepipe, where the temperature was a few degrees cooler than on the coast, or—

'Hello,' a light voice called, breaking into her thoughts, and she saw Choo's mother walking around the side of the house.

She grinned. Amy Yap was a bright, sociable young woman and a good neighbour. Delighted that her daughter had found a new friend, she had wasted no time in inviting her and Harriet round for a drink and a chat. And since that first meeting they had spent other happy afternoons together. Amy wanted to ask her and Lorcan to dinner but, she had explained, her husband was currently short of staff at his restaurant and could not take time off. However, as soon as he had a free evening, Harriet must come and sleep over, while the four adults enjoyed a meal.

'That's so cute. You've caught the spirit exactly,' Amy enthused, peering over her shoulder at the sketch. 'Would you do one for me? I'll pay, of course.'

Jess climbed to her feet. 'You can have this when it's finished, but there's no charge to friends.'

The Chinese woman smiled. 'Thanks. Choo, it's time to go home,' she called.

'Not yet,' came the protest.

'Now. Wash yourself off and find your sandals. Have you drawn any pictures of Lorcan?' Amy asked as the little girl sloshed her hands around in the paddling pool.

She shook her head. 'None.'

'Why not? He's gorgeous.' There was a mischievous twinkle of almond-shaped eyes. 'He must be heaven to live with. Come along, Choo.'

As mother and daughter disappeared, Jess sighed. Although Amy had been told she was Harriet's nanny, she had apparently decided that she and Lorcan were lovers. Should she explain that if her nanny duties lacked a certain validity it was because she was really a bodyguard? She wrinkled her nose. It seemed unlikely the explanation would make one iota of difference.

'Can I play for a bit longer?' Harriet appealed. 'Please?'

'For ten minutes,' she said, closing her sketchpad and heading into the kitchen to collect scissors.

Because the house had looked so bare, she had filled vases with flowers and spread them around. The atmosphere had been instantly brightened, but now fresh flowers were required. Wandering from a crimson hibiscus bush to a clump of white lilies, to other tropical blooms which grew in the attractively overgrown garden, Jess started to cut a selection.

Her sense of danger from kidnappers remained nonexistent, she reflected as she snipped. There had never been a hint of anyone watching or following Harriet and no further threat had been received; so the kidnapper, or airhead, was not in the business of applying pressure. Indeed, she was beginning to feel that they must have lost interest and her presence was superfluous.

Did Lorcan truly believe that his daughter might be abducted? The signals which came from him contradicted and she could not decide. Jess chewed at her lip. She still had a nagging suspicion he was keeping something from her and not revealing the truth, the whole truth.

She had stretched down to snip off a low sprig of bougainvillea when the kitchen door suddenly banged. Looking behind her, she saw Lorcan coming down the steps, his brow sleeked with sweat and dusty in his work clothes. As their eyes met, she straightened. She had been bending with her backside stuck up in the air and her bikini pants were high-cut and scanty.

'You're an hour early,' she protested, inspecting her watch.

'We finished the main job in hand, so I let everyone go and came home.'

'A good idea. You look whacked.'

Lorcan raked the swathe of dark hair back from his brow. 'I've not been sleeping too well,' he said curtly, and frowned at Harriet. 'What on earth do you think you're doing?'

As Jess followed his gaze, her eyes opened wide. When the little girl had been making pies with Choo the mud had been restricted mainly to their hands, but now the front of her was plastered from shoulder to knee. During her flower-gathering, Harriet had been busy.

'I'm playing at squelchy squilchy,' the child said, scooping up the remains of the last pie and giggling as thick brown sludge oozed out between her fingers. 'Senga would never've let me play like this. She didn't want me to get dirty. Neither would Grandma, but Jess—'

'She's willing to let you do whatever you want?' Lorcan demanded.

Hearing his disapproval, Harriet pouted. 'I like playing squelchy squilchy. Wommie likes it too.'

'Forget about Wommie,' he snapped. 'I'm sick to death of you prattling on about that stupid—'

'The mud'll wash off,' Jess cut in, and indicated the coil of the garden hose. 'I'll spray Harriet—'

'Goody!' the little girl shouted.

'—and afterwards I'll take her into my shower with me. So if you want to go and have your shower—' She looked pointedly towards the house.

He glowered, looking very intense, very Irish, very moody. 'Yes, ma'am,' he said, after a moment, and strode away.

If Lorcan had come home at his usual time, he would not have seen Harriet's mud coating and he would not have caught *her* in her bikini, Jess thought as they sat together on the back veranda after dinner that evening. Although she often wore it in the afternoons, she always made sure she was dressed for his return. It seemed easier on both their nervous systems. But the bikini had been the spur for his irritation. Finding her so scantily clad would have hit him with a reminder of how he had desired her. And still did. So he had been impatient with her and had shouted at his daughter.

'Did you never play with mud when you were a child?' she asked.

Lorcan frowned. 'Not that I can remember.'

'Playing with mud or Plasticine or doing finger painting and such is good for you.'

'How do you work that out?'

'It stimulates the joy of touch and releases the inhibitions, which, in turn, enriches a person's sex life as an adult.'

'You read that in a women's magazine somewhere?'

She nodded. 'But it makes sense to me.'

'So when Harriet grows up she's going to be an unending delight to her partner because today you encouraged her to take a mud bath?' he enquired pithily.

'I didn't encourage her. She coated herself without my realising. However, yes, that's the theory.'

'And because I didn't spend three-quarters of my childhood rolling around in the stuff I'm repressed?'

Her smile was mechanical. 'You said it, not me.'

'Whereas you were a mud addict and now—' his blue eyes clashed with hers '—you're red-hot in bed?'

'White-hot,' Jess declared, and swallowed. Why she should have launched into a diatribe about sexual mores she had no idea, but it was having a disastrous effect on her composure. 'You shouldn't let Harriet's talk about Wommie get to you,' she said, desperate to change the subject.

'I guess not.' Lorcan took a mouthful of the local Green Island white rum which, now that the duty-free whisky had been consumed, he drank in the evenings. 'I think the reason it does is—' He stopped to frown. 'Harriet's moved around so much she's never had a chance to make real-life long-lasting friends and so she's invented a pretend one. It makes me feel guilty—' his frown deepened '—hellish guilty, because it's *my* fault that she's been uprooted.'

'I always lived in the same house and had plenty of long-term friends, but when I was little I also had a make-believe companion,' she told him.

'You did?' he said, in surprise.

'She was called Gloria Delphine.'

He looked amused. 'Gloria Delphine?'

'I thought it was the most classy name and she was extremely snooty, turned up her nose at everything from sausages to face-washing to ballet lessons. All the things which didn't appeal to me. But lots of kids go through the "pretend friend" stage. It's nothing unusual.'

'Really?'

Jess nodded. 'Really. So you've no need to worry about it nor to feel guilty.'

'Thanks, from now on I won't.' Smiling, he took a reflective taste of rum. 'I meant to tell you, Sir Peter rang me today. He and Gerard'll be stopping off here next weekend on their way down to South Africa where they have some business. On Saturday they want to visit the site to check on progress, talk over costs et cetera, so would you be willing to look after Harriet while I'm with them?'

'No problem,' she said, seeing her weekend away disappear.

'And Sir Peter suggested that on Sunday we all go out on a boat together.'

'Including me?'

'Especially you. You don't think Gerard would miss a chance to see you in a bikini, do you?' he asked, his tone sardonic. 'You're happy to come along?'

'Very,' Jess replied.

When keeping guard at the play-school, she had often watched boats sail out from the harbour and wished that she could be aboard. And if she was unable to go off on her own this weekend she could do so the next.

'What I thought I'd do is hire a catamaran with a crew,' Lorcan continued. 'I'll arrange for them to take us along the coast where we can get a view of the hotel from the sea, stop someplace for lunch, and have time to swim or snorkel or simply sunbathe in the afternoon.'

'Sounds great,' she said.

Jess smiled beneath the brim of her straw boater. She was sitting cross-legged in the prow of one of the catamaran's twin hulls, watching the coastline unravel in an endless green ribbon of forested hills. The sun felt warm on her bare back, a light breeze swelled the sail, there was a gentle swishing of waves as the boat skimmed across the deep blue waters.

All of a sudden, her smile subsided. The noxious smell of a cheroot was seeping into her nostrils. It was the smell which had lingered on her clothes after her visit to the Warwick offices and one which she felt sure she would recognise anywhere. It was a smell which warned that Gerard was arriving to chat. Again.

'Pity I'm here for such a short visit,' the young man said, squatting down on the deck beside her. He placed a hand on her arm, as if to indicate that he understood her distress at such a brief meeting and was offering comfort. 'But we shall be stopping over for the weekend on our return journey in a couple of weeks' time.'

'Mmm,' Jess murmured, reminding herself of Naseem and deciding that that would be the weekend when she went away.

After making a beeline for her at the harbour that morning, Gerard had paid constant attention; and he had not improved on a second meeting. His love affair with himself remained undisturbed. He still laughed loudly, usually at his own jokes. He continued to be too familiar. She stared out at the ocean which sparkled like diamonds in the sunshine. Though she must take some responsibility for the latter.

'My word, you look good, my dear,' Sir Peter had said appreciatively, when she had climbed out of the Cherokee in a white mini sundress which she wore over a matching bikini.

'Good enough to eat,' Gerard had declared, with the habitual guffaw.

Lorcan had not said a word—as he had made no comment on her appearance back at the house, either.

His silence had annoyed her—with her tan and long legs she *did* look good and a compliment would have been no more than courteous—so, in a fit of pique, she had devoted herself to Gerard.

As they had sailed off across the lagoon, she had laughed at his sledgehammer wit, shown a keen interest in his views, gazed at him as if he were the most exciting man she had come across in years. He was not. The designer logos which smothered his red and yellow striped vest and shorts might indicate a hefty price tag and a fashion-conscious intention to thrill, but add the gelled hair, white-cheese pallor, plus the beginnings of a paunch like his father's, and he did not excite her. It was Lorcan, lean in frayed denim shorts and with his dark hair tousled by the breeze, who did that. Jess hoisted up the strap of her bikini. Much to her irritation.

But now Gerard was in continual pursuit. It did not matter that her devotion had lasted just the short five minutes it had taken her to realise her folly—after which she had become far more circumspect—he continued to pay court. And he seemed to take it for granted that his attentions were welcomed because she was smitten with him. And had been smitten since the first time they had met.

'I must put more sun lotion on Harriet,' she declared, looking back towards the stern where the little girl was sitting with Lorcan and Sir Peter.

As she stood up, the young man clasped a possessive hand around her ankle. A hand which Jess longed to kick away. 'Come back soon, babe,' he purred.

Babe? She winced. He sounded like a gangster from an old-time B movie.

After applying some unnecessary lotion to Harriet's arms, legs and nose, she sat down beside Sir Peter.

'You're pleased with the hotel?' she asked.

She knew he was pleased. Lorcan had reported back last night that he was delighted and the businessman's praise when they had sailed past the site earlier had been awash with superlatives. But she needed an excuse to avoid returning to his son.

'Overjoyed,' Sir Peter proclaimed and, repeating many of the superlatives, he expressed his pleasure again. 'Lorcan is doing a fantastic job,' he said, turning to beam at him. 'He—'

'Can we go and sit on the front for a bit, Daddy?' Harriet appealed.

Lorcan nodded, seeming as eager to escape yet another paean of praise as his daughter. 'If you'll excuse us?'

'Go ahead,' the older man said benignly, and as they made their way down the boat he embarked on a lengthy list of Lorcan's talents. 'Charles Sohan is pea-green that we managed to grab him, but he's become pragmatic. What will be, will be.'

'So you don't believe Mr Sohan was responsible for the note?' Jess enquired.

'No. We happened to meet at a business awards luncheon last week and I took the opportunity of mentioning it to him. Didn't say Gerard'd felt sure he'd been the perpetrator,' he said, casting a glance towards the prow where Harriet had commandeered his son and was singing, her high child's voice carrying in the breeze.

The song was one she had learned at play-school and featured the dodo, a gigantic turkey-like bird, which had once tramped the shores of Mauritius but was now extinct. After singing it repeatedly at home and to Sir Peter, Harriet had sung it, individually, to each of the three Creole youths who crewed the catamaran. Everyone had dutifully listened and given suitable praise, which was just as well because Gerard looked truculent and bored stiff.

'Sohan reckoned the note must've been the work of some dimwit out to cause a spot of bother,' Sir Peter continued, 'and belonged in the waste-paper basket.'

'Which is what Lorcan said.'

'Initially, but later when he asked for you to be employed I realised he had genuine fears.'

Her brow crinkled. 'Lorcan asked for me?'

'He did. I'd accepted that there probably wasn't any danger, but out of the blue and at the last minute, as you know—' she received a sympathetic smile '—he telephoned to say he thought a bodyguard would be a wise precaution, after all. Didn't want him to be worried, so I was happy to go along with his request and to foot the bill. He was keen to pay for you himself, but I insisted.' Sir Peter looked along the boat to where one of the crew was talking to Lorcan. 'Do you think he's worried? He seems a little on edge to me.'

Jess pulled the straw hat lower over her brow. 'Probably pressure of work,' she said dismissively.

'And you haven't noticed anything out of the ordinary to make you think the threat could've been serious?'

'Not a thing.'

'We're going to pull in for lunch,' Lorcan announced, coming towards them past the white sail. He pointed to a small secluded bay which had an arc of silver sand, a tumble of rocks to one side and was edged by palm trees. 'There.'

Sir Peter patted his stomach. 'About time,' he said, with a smile. 'All this sea air has made me hungry.'

The catamaran was anchored close to shore and, with Lorcan carrying Harriet on his shoulders, everyone waded in through the shallows. The crew followed, laden with trays of crockery and cutlery, cool-boxes, foil-wrapped dishes and other supplies. Several journeys were needed. A red checked tablecloth was spread over a rough-sawn table which sat with benches in the shade—the bay was a favourite stopping place, one of the youths explained—and cold lobster, prawns, smoked marlin and bowls of salad stuffs were set out.

'What's that?' Harriet asked suspiciously as another dish appeared.

'Heart of palm or "millionaire's salad",' Jess told her, and grinned. 'It's delicious, though I don't think you'll like it.'

A small chin angled upwards. 'Yes, I will.'

Harriet liked everything and ate well, and so did the rest of the party. Fruit juice, chilled beer or wine accompanied the food and there was a choice of fresh fruit for dessert: mango, papaya or small sweet finger bananas.

When the meal was finished, the crew cleared away, declared an hour's siesta and went back to the boat.

'Time for a zizz,' Sir Peter said, lying down on the sand in the shade.

'We don't want to disturb him,' Lorcan whispered to Harriet as the older man began to snore gently, 'so how about we look for pieces of coral to add to your collection?'

'Yes, please,' the child said, and they went off along the beach.

'We'll go for a walk,' declared Gerard, and, grabbing hold of Jess's hand, he drew her with him from the table and in the opposite direction.

After a few yards, she pulled her hand free. 'Too sticky,' she said.

With her escort telling her about other tropical islands he had visited and boasting about how he *always* stayed at the most élite resorts and travelled first class, they walked to the end of the bay. Once or twice he stumbled, which she felt was due to his liberal consumption of wine.

'This way,' he announced as they started to retrace their steps and, making another abrupt grab for her hand, he hauled her up the slope of sand, beneath the low-hanging branches of a tree and into a hidden glade.

A window of opportunity had been recognised and entered.

'I don't—' Jess started to protest, but he had dropped down, tugging her with him.

'Alone at last,' Gerard crooned, and leant forward to kiss her.

She veered back. As his father's employee and a representative of Citadel Security, she had no wish to quarrel with him—which was why she had hesitated to object about being manhandled before—but neither did she want to kiss him. No, thanks. The sight of those puckered, blubbery lips was making her shudder.

'Sorry,' she said, smiling and shifting away, 'I'm not interested.'

He gave a smug chuckle. 'Playing Miss Demure, are we? It ain't going to work. I know when a woman wants me and you're in for a treat, babe, because I have an advanced degree in the erotic arts,' he declared, and lunged, knocking her hat askew.

This time, she spread-eagled both hands on his chest and pushed him away. Hard. Her arms straight out. 'I am not interested,' she repeated, biting out the words, then, feeling it might be politic to soften the rebuff, added, 'Not in anyone.'

The young man looked at her, his face an angry puce, his grey eyes cold, his mouth pinched. His position as his father's only son and heir meant refusals were rare and he was not a good loser.

'You're interested in Lorcan,' he declared.

Jess readjusted the angle of her hat. Was her fascination so obvious? 'No,' she said.

'You damn well are. I've seen how you look at him. I know you've got the serious hots for the guy. Tough luck, you're wasting your time,' Gerard said nastily. 'Our architect friend is still hooked up on his wife. Two years seems a fair stretch of time in which to come to terms, and some folk recover sooner, but there are those who spend the rest of their lives grieving over the loss of their true love. Like Lorcan,' he thrust.

Something seemed to pierce inside her. 'Yes.'

'As soon as they met he couldn't wait to marry her,' the young man declared, recognising that he had touched a nerve and gloating over it, 'and who can blame him? She was a stunner. A real prize. You know she was the daughter of Tony Rocca?'

'Tony Rocca, the Hollywood film director?' Jess said, in surprise.

'That's him—the dashing Italian stud who's had heaven knows how many wives. Sara and Lorcan wasted no time in sealing their love with that ultimate sign of devotion, a baby. Just a tragedy they had only two years together before the beautiful creature went out in her car one day and—crump.'

'She died in a road accident?'

'Smashed into a tree. So remember, even if he should fancy you Lorcan will always belong to the delicious Sara. She has shackled his broken heart.' Having made his spiteful and somewhat florid point, Gerard climbed to his feet, brushed sand from his designer shorts and dipped low beneath the branches. 'Wait for the endgame, babe,' he threw back.

'Excuse me?' she said, not understanding, but he had disappeared.

Jess followed slowly. At the subconscious level she supposed she had known that Lorcan was still captivated by his wife. His reluctance to speak about her and the tightness which gripped him whenever she was mentioned indicated a lasting hurt. He had not recovered from her death and continued to mourn, continued to suffer, continued to love.

Even so, to hear Gerard spell it out loud and clear had been unsettling. Why? she wondered. If Lorcan remained enthralled, why should it bother her? Her shoulders were squared. It didn't. She might be attracted by the physical aspects of the man, but she had no designs on his heart and soul.

Back at the table, Sir Peter was awake and refreshed, and admiring fragments of coral which Harriet was busily explaining would be included in the display which she and Jess had arranged on the living-room windowsills. Lorcan was standing nearby, gazing out at the ocean as he drank a cold beer.

As they wandered up, he turned. 'Been exploring?' he said.

'We have,' Gerard replied, and gave a snide smile. 'Most stimulating it was, too.'

'I can imagine,' he rasped.

Jess looked at the two men. Gerard had purposefully given the impression that they had shared some intimate moments during their absence, and by his surly response Lorcan had indicated his disapproval. Whilst the deception rankled, she could not deny that there was a certain satisfaction in knowing he felt aggrieved.

Although the next time he spoke his tone was amiable she detected a thread of steel in his voice and, as the afternoon progressed, she became aware that his patience with Gerard was growing gossamer-thin. It was clear that, like her, Lorcan did not wish to fall out with his paymaster's son—nor alert Sir Peter to his irritation—yet at times he looked as if he would dearly love to strangle him.

* * *

'Gerard got on your nerves today?' Jess enquired lightly as she went down the back steps and out to the washing whirly.

It was nine-thirty p.m. The catamaran had docked late in the afternoon and they had driven the visitors back to their hotel. An hour later, and after a snack which Sir Peter had insisted they must have in the coffee-shop, they had ferried them on to the airport to catch their plane. Returning home, Harriet had been bathed and put to bed. Salt-sticky from swimming, both of them had showered and changed—and Jess had rinsed out her bikini.

Lorcan had been leaning against the balustrade of the veranda with a nightcap glass of rum in his hand, but as she spoke he straightened.

'He did, and so did you,' he said, frowning down at her through the shadows.

Lights from the house cast pale yellow circles on the nearest part of the garden, while moonlight dappled the remainder in silver and black.

'Me?'

'The way you flirted with him, fluttering your eyelashes and hanging on his every word, was—' his nostrils flared '—sickening! OK, the guy must have some appeal, though I'm damned if I can figure out what it is, but why you should make eyes and then disappear with him into the undergrowth for a—a canoodle amazes me! I thought you had better judgement than to go off with—'

'Are you jealous?' Jess enquired.

'Jealous of that obnoxious little squirt? Give me a break.'

She pegged up her bikini. 'You sound as if you're jealous.'

'No way. I just can't understand what it is about him which attracts you.'

Her hand in the pocket of the jeans she wore with a cut-off top, Jess sauntered towards him. 'Perhaps it's his sense of humour?' she suggested.

Lorcan swore ripely.

'Or his poetic, sensitive side?'

'Chance'd be a fine thing.'

'Or his young good looks?'

'The guy may only be twenty-six, but he's already gone to seed bodywise and chances are he'll be bald before the year's out.'

'Who ever said women were bitchy?' she remarked, walking up the steps and onto the veranda beside him. 'Nothing about Gerard attracts me. I think he's obnoxious, too.'

He slung her a suspicious look. 'So why flirt with him?'

'It was an error of judgement,' she said carelessly, 'but I didn't go off with him on purpose. Or into the undergrowth. And when he tried to kiss me I stopped him.'

'You applied a knee to a sensitive part of his anatomy?'

'No, I just pushed him away.'

'Pity,' Lorcan said darkly.

'It was effective, though Gerard didn't take it too well.'

Jess recalled how malicious the young man had been, then another thought intruded. 'Earlier when I was talking to Sir Peter he told me you'd requested a bodyguard,' she said.

He drank from his glass. 'So?'

'You reckoned you'd decided to go along with his wishes in order to please him.'

'Did I?' Turning from her, he looked out into the garden. 'Possibly, though what difference does it make which of us decided to hire you?'

'It makes a big difference,' she said, forced to speak to his back. 'It means you changed your mind for a specific reason.'

'Like what?'

'I don't know, but I do know when you're being evasive. Like now, so I'm going to bed.' Jess marched towards the kitchen, but in the open doorway she stopped. 'You don't believe Mr Sohan had any connection with the note, but I bet you have an idea about who could've sent it.'

Lorcan turned to face her. 'I don't.'

'Ha, ha,' she jibed, and stalked indoors.

'It's true,' he protested, following her.

She spun round to confront him. 'In that case, why did you change your mind and request security for Harriet, and only Harriet, at the very last minute and why—?'

Her words stopped. He had caught hold of her by the hips, lifted her up and sat her down on the kitchen table.

'Being grilled by you after a long day in the sun is not good for my blood pressure,' he grated.

Jess took a breath. He was leaning over her at a dangerous angle from the hip. Leaning close.

'You have blood in your veins?' she said. 'I thought it was iced water. But why—?'

'Do you never take no for an answer?'

'Rarely. If something seems odd I ask questions and keep on asking until I get satisfactory answers. Your

answers are not satisfactory. I may be a humble
bodyguard, but—'

'I don't think "humble" is the right word,' Lorcan
said, and, standing closer, he stretched down his arms
and put his hands flat on the table, one on either side
of her. 'How about aggressive?'

'I'll settle for assertive, but—'

She stopped short, needing to take another breath.
His nearness was doing strange things to her pulse
rate. The chemistry was kicking in again.

'Aggressive,' he repeated.

'Shut up,' she said, and she kissed him.

It was just a brief dab on his lips, but when she
drew back her heart was hammering like a drum. After
a month of no contact, what crazy impulse had suddenly made her do that? she wondered.

'Lust never sleeps,' Lorcan muttered.

'Excuse me?'

'Old folk wisdom. But if you're going to shut me
up at least do it properly. Kiss me properly.'

Jess looked at him. He had laid down a challenge
and she would accept it, she thought defiantly. She
was not going to succumb to the jitters and
back down.

'Yes, my liege,' she said, and kissed him again.

As their mouths met there was a moment of hesitation, then the kiss took on a life of its own. A fe-
vered life. A thrilling life. Lips parted, tongues
touched, they tasted each other. The kiss went on and
on, and when at last they separated both of them were
breathing heavily.

'Now we make love,' Lorcan said.

Excitement surged, a traitorous excitement which
she rapidly quelled. 'Until you decide to stop?'

He ran the tip of his finger across the bare tanned midriff which was revealed between her cut-off top and her jeans, awakening all the nerve-ends. 'I won't stop.'

'You've acquired the necessary protection?' she enquired coolly.

'No, but you're on the Pill.'

'You believe me?'

'I do and I realise that you'd never take foolish chances.'

Jess frowned. Whilst it was good to know that his opinion of her had been redeemed, it did not mean that she would jump through his hoops. She was not going to obligingly co-operate and do what he desired.

'Thanks for the vote of confidence,' she said. 'However, I don't want to make love.'

Lorcan drew his knuckles along the curve of her cheek. 'Yes, you do,' he said softly. 'Jess, for four weeks we've both been going silently insane wanting each other. Do you honestly believe we can last out another two months? There is no chance. Sooner or later, you and I are going to wind up in bed together.' He ran his hand down the column of her neck, over the swell of her breast, to the silken skin of her midriff. 'I've tried to resist you. God knows, I've tried, but it's impossible.'

As his fingers caressed her skin, she felt the sweet, sharp ache of need. 'So—so we might as well get it over with?' she asked jerkily.

He smiled. 'A romantic at heart,' he said, and kissed her again.

She did not protest. What he desired, she desired. As he said, their making love had become inevitable.

When her breathing had quickened and her hazel eyes were misty with desire, he drew the cut-off top over her head.

'Like ripe plums,' he murmured, gazing at her naked breasts and their prominent peaks. 'I want to pluck.' He touched a finger to a tightening nipple, making her clench her teeth. 'I want to suck.'

Lorcan lowered his head and she leant back, offering her breasts to him. As she felt the lap of his tongue and the pull of his mouth, she cried out in a shocked animal cry of arousal. Fisting her fingers into the thick dark hair on the top of his head, she drew him closer. He was tasting her nipple, teasing it with his tongue and creating glorious tweaks of sensation which were multiplying inside her.

'Again,' Jess begged, wondering what had happened to her modesty, to her inhibitions, wondering how she could be so brazen. 'Again.'

He raised his head. His blue eyes were slumberous and his grin twisted. 'You want me to take you on the kitchen table?' he said.

'Anywhere.'

'Maybe another time, but for now I'd prefer us to make love in a little more comfort.' Curving an arm around her, he lifted her onto her feet. 'How about in your bed?'

She nodded.

Somewhere amongst walking them through and kissing her, he dispensed with the rest of her clothes and with his. She had been right, Jess thought dizzily; he was of Greek god proportions. They lay down and as she felt the fiery thrust of his manhood against her her heartbeat quickened.

'For the past month, I've been wanting to look at you again,' Lorcan said, his gaze feasting on the high globes of her breasts, the smooth plane of her belly, the corn-coloured curls which grew at her thighs. Raising his hand, he ran it slowly down the centre of her body until he cupped her and felt the source of her heat. 'White-hot,' he murmured.

She rested her forehead on his shoulder. 'Only with you.'

He kissed her again. 'I want to taste more of you, all of you,' he told her.

Her fingers clutched tight at his shoulders as he moved slowly down her body, the touch of his mouth igniting a thousand tiny flares of need. He clasped his long fingers around one firm breast and lowered his mouth. As he suckled at the sensitive peak, contractions tightened in the base of her stomach and Jess shuddered and cried out.

An ache was pulsing, and when he slid lower and she felt the probe of his tongue at the core of her she cried out again, lost in a whirl of emotions. Placing his hands on her thighs, he gave himself the freedom to inhale her feminine scent and to savour the musky juices. The ache throbbed and she writhed beneath him, whimpering deep in her throat.

Lorcan brought himself up beside her on the pillow and his hand slid over her, exploring here, lingering there, as he tormented them both. The knot of desire tightened and she strained closer. The rock-hard press of his body against hers made her feel as if she was drinking in air, walking on air, and two steps from heaven.

Wanting to please him as he pleased her, she slid her hand down between them.

'Dear God, Jess,' he groaned as her fingers curled around him, and when she slid down to his thighs he closed his eyes and his head fell back. 'Jess,' he said again, in a hoarse voice.

When he could submit to the pleasuring no longer, he drew her up beside him and straddled her. Hard and hot, like liquid fire, he slid into her.

'Open your eyes,' he commanded, and when she looked at him she saw a fierceness in his face which should have frightened her, but which filled her heart with joy. She had *this* effect on him? 'I wanted to make it last,' Lorcan said raggedly. 'But I can't wait...it's been so long since...you excite me so much.'

Jess wrapped an arm around his neck. Whatever his needs, she knew she could satisfy them. Wherever he led, she would follow.

'Don't wait,' she told him. 'I'm ready. So ready.'

He moved and as their bodies rocked in a compulsive rhythm she clung to him. He was taking her to somewhere higher and harder than she had ever been before. To a place where all was throbbing need and urgent desire...and bliss.

'Lorcan,' she said, his name ending on a breath.

For a moment he held himself rigid, then he moved again, his hips bucking. He shuddered, trembled. Their desire fused, exploded—and together they plunged headlong into the soft dark oblivion of fulfilment.

CHAPTER SIX

LORCAN'S decision to include a large swimming pool within the hotel village had been a shrewd one, Jess thought as she floated idly on her back. Because Mauritius was almost completely encircled by one of the world's finest coral reefs, tranquil lagoons edged the shore. Like here, down the lane from the house. And whilst the shallow sea bed was conveniently safe for children and made it easy to watch the antics of shoals of tiny fluorescent fish it eliminated any hope of serious swimming.

Raising her head, she looked out to where a thin white line separated the pale turquoise of the lagoon from the deep blue ocean. She wished she could swim seriously now, as she did most days at home. She longed to power through the water, limbs working, adrenaline pumping, stretching her body to the limit and emptying her mind.

Her gaze swung to the sand. Harriet and Choo had dug a large hole and were rushing back and forth to the water with their buckets, attempting to fill it. The task seemed destined to last for ever, so while they were busy should she slip off for a swim? Jess paddled her feet. Her professionalism said no. The odds on someone swooping down and snatching up her small charge might appear to have dwindled to a thousand to one, yet a dogged sense of duty insisted she stay close. She stared up at the sky through her dark glasses. Her mind remained full—full of Lorcan and

how for the past ten nights he had come into her bed
and they had made love.

As her thoughts travelled back to the previous
evening, Jess felt her nipples tighten and an ache pulse
between her thighs. Lorcan had once spoken of a
'torrid' affair, and their lovemaking was hot and
highly charged. One kiss and they fell upon each other,
feverishly tugging off clothes and devouring each
other. It seemed that every night both of them wanted
more and both gave more. She had never felt such
quick, urgent greed for a man. Never needed to
possess and be possessed with such intensity. Never
realised that passion could be so adventurous,
uninhibited, wonderful.

Yet, after their passion, every night her lover returned to his own room and his own bed. And every
time she felt bereft.

Jess flippered with her hands. She was being foolish.
As well as taking a caring consideration of Harriet's
feelings, his nightly departure helped emphasise the
fact that all they were involved in was a sexual liaison,
pure and simple. She had been aware that that was
what Lorcan offered and, by making love with him
the first time, had accepted his terms and agreed. In
any case, an affair with no strings attached was what
she wanted. Her painting ambitions allowed no time
or space in her life for commitment, either. Not right
now. Not yet. So when she left the island their involvement would end.

She sighed. It was such a *sizzling* involvement. At
his touch, her skin burned. And he touched in so many
delicious places. Touched with his fingers, his mouth,
his tongue. Jess took a breath. Whoa, girl. As it was
their lovemaking started earlier and lasted longer each
evening, but if she allowed her thoughts to continue

unchecked there was a danger she might leap on Lorcan the moment he came in through the door. That would never do. In Harriet's presence, their relationship was strictly platonic. For the child's sake, they never said or did anything which hinted at intimacy.

Lowering her feet to the sea floor, she pushed herself up, standing knee-deep in the water.

'Time to go, kids,' she called, and smiled at the usual barrage of protests.

As Jess waded carefully towards the shore—step on a coral shard and it could be painful—a light dazzled in her eye. She blinked, momentarily blinded. What was that? Peering into the depths of the casuarina trees which backed the beach, she saw two youths. Both wore pale linen jackets, dark open-necked shirts and shiny pipe-leg trousers, outfits which erred on the side of flash. One was a brawny Creole with short dreadlocks dangling over his brow, while the other was a reed-thin, rather bouffant-haired Indian. He wore a medallion around his neck and it was this which had glinted in the sunshine.

She frowned behind her sunglasses. She did not recognise them—nor the beat-up Toyota which was parked further back on the road—but could they be members of what she privately and somewhat wearily called her 'fan club'?

Because the village lay off the beaten track and did not attract too many tourists, her daily presence beside the harbour had been a novelty. And as a tall young blonde she was a rarity. A crowd-pulling rarity for often when she went to purchase her morning drink a group of youths gathered to watch her approach, and her retreat. Sometimes one would attempt to strike up a conversation, which she always politely curtailed. The young men were harmless, but she did not want to encourage them. She preferred to devote her mornings to her painting.

This far, her admirers had confined themselves to the harbour, but the Creole youth had his eyes fixed on her and seemed to be making a comment about her to his companion. Jess groaned. She did not enjoy being observed in the mornings and she hoped she was not going to be targeted in the afternoons, too.

Telling Harriet and Choo to get ready to leave, she quickly dried herself and tied a kanga over her bikini. When she looked into the whispering casuarinas again, both the youths and the Toyota had gone.

'Wait for me at the kerb,' she instructed as the two little girls skipped off ahead of her towards the road. 'What do you do?' she enquired, joining them a minute or so later where they obediently stood.

'Look right, look left,' they chanted, looking both ways, 'and if the road is clear—cross.'

As usual there was no traffic in sight, so they crossed over and walked up the lane.

'It's so good of you to look after Choo,' Amy said, when she delivered home her daughter.

'That's OK, she's no trouble,' Jess replied, smiling at the child. 'You had a busy afternoon at the restaurant?'

'Busy and so useful. Michael's still short-staffed, but I was able to prepare a whole heap of vegetables. That dinner date with you and Lorcan, and Harriet sleeping over, will happen some time,' her neighbour continued, 'though I still can't say when.'

'Don't worry about it.'

'Couldn't Harriet sleep over tonight?' Choo appealed.

'Yes, I can,' Harriet said delightedly.

Amy looked at Jess. 'I'm happy if you are.'

She hesitated. The bodyguard rulebook must advise against sanctioning such a separation, but was there a danger? She could not see any. And yet rules were rules.

'Please, Jess,' Harriet appealed, gazing up at her with big blue eyes. 'Please.'

She sighed. She was a push-over. 'It's fine by me, though—'

'Goody!' the child yelled.

'Yippee!' Choo shouted. 'Can Harriet have her dinner with us, too?'

'And breakfast in the morning,' Amy said, setting off yet more shrieks of joy.

Grinning, Jess put her hands over her ears. She had been about to say that, whilst she agreed, the arrangement should be cleared with Lorcan; but the moment had gone. However, she felt sure he would not object.

As she returned to the bungalow with Harriet to supervise a hasty bath and pack her overnight things, she was pensive. Ten days ago, she had said that if something seemed odd she kept asking questions, but their lovemaking had knocked any questions out of her head. So she had yet to discover whether Lorcan truly believed his daughter might be under threat of kidnap and, if so, from whom.

After returning Harriet to her lodgings, she saw the departing Naseem out of the house and went to shower. She was putting on a pink button-through dress when the telephone rang in the hall.

'It's me,' Lorcan said, when she answered it.

Her heart performed a loop the loop. 'Hello.'

'I'm afraid I'm tied up with a job and going to be late. Can't say when I'll be back, but have dinner without me.'

'Will do. By the way, Harriet's spending the night at Choo's. I said it'd be all right.'

'She's staying next door?' he demanded.

Jess frowned. His voice had sharpened. Did he think she had made the wrong decision? Might he believe she was shirking her duty and there could be a danger?

'You don't approve?'

'On the contrary I'm all for it, but I'm amazed. She's never agreed to stay with a friend before. In fact, on the occasions when it's been mooted, she's become weepy and clingy and refused point-blank.'

'Harriet was desperate to go,' she told him, and described her excitement.

'This is thanks to you,' Lorcan said. 'Since you've been around Harriet's kind of…steadied. She has far fewer tantrums and seems more contented. But I must go.' His voice deepened, taking on a huskiness. 'See you later, Jess.'

Her pulse rate quickened. She knew what he was thinking about and what 'later' meant—the two of them, in bed.

'See you,' she said.

If the little girl was more contented, so was her father, Jess mused as she ate dinner, a prawn salad, in the kitchen later. Over the past week and a half, Lorcan had visibly relaxed. He whistled, sang snatches of songs, smiled a lot. He must also be sleeping better, for he no longer came back from the site exhausted. Their lovemaking appeared to have given him new energy, new stamina, new ease. He was a man with reasons to be cheerful.

Now that her sexual needs were being so marvellously satisfied, she ought to be feeling easier, too, she brooded as she finished her meal. The dirty dishes were carried over to the sink. On one level she was, yet on another—

Jess narrowed her eyes. Something had moved behind the hibiscus bush. She squinted, looking closer. The dying evening sun flamed the garden and cast long black shadows, but through the interweave of branches she could see two silhouetted figures.

'Damn!' she said, recognising the paleness of a jacket.

They were the youths who had been at the beach earlier. They must have followed her back to the house in the hope of catching another sight of her in her bikini or, perhaps, undressing.

Stepping back from the window and out of sight, she frowned. She was jumping to conclusions. The duo might seem like peeping Toms, but there was also the possibility that they might be kidnappers. OK, it appeared unlikely—if they had been hanging around surely they must have seen her take Harriet next door?—yet it should not be dismissed out of hand. And if they were she was not going to miss out on a chance to detain them and thus prove to Lorcan that she was a worthy protector of his daughter!

Jess frowned. She needed to know whether their interest was centred on her or the little girl, so she would set a trap. She would open the back door, lie low and wait. If the youths ventured into the house, it followed that they were involved in something more serious than ogling.

But what would she do with them if they *did* come inside? She looked around. A yard or two across from the door was a walk-in cupboard where mops, brooms, the vacuum cleaner and such were stored. The intruders could be locked in there while she rang for the police.

After opening the cupboard in preparation, she unfastened the back door and left it ajar. Crouching down beside the sink, Jess waited. Damn, she had forgotten to get her pepper spray and it was too late now. For five minutes nothing happened. She was about to abandon her ploy—which smacked of the *too* obvious—when something moved outside. She peeped out. Obvious or not, the bait had been taken. The youths were treading cautiously onto the veranda, the Indian one in front. They must be kidnappers. And now she would show Lorcan that she was a true professional and worth every penny which Sir Peter had paid!

As the Indian boy took a first tentative step into the kitchen, she leapt up, pushed at his back and propelled him helter-skelter into the open cupboard. Swivelling, she grabbed for his companion who was dithering—should he attempt a rescue or run away?—and heaved him in, too. Slamming the door, she turned the key in the lock.

'Simple!' she said delightedly.

As protesting shouts of Creole, the pidgin French used on the island, started to sound and fists were thumped, she eyed the door. The youths were pounding with some force; would it hold while the police were summoned? She lodged a kitchen chair beneath the knob. It would now.

Dashing into the hall, Jess lifted the receiver. She had begun to dial when she heard the tread of footsteps—firm male footsteps approaching the front door. She froze. A shiver ran down her spine. For a split second, it seemed as if she had miscalculated and there were three of them. How would she cope with three? *Could* she cope?

But as a key turned in the lock she realised that the footsteps had belonged to Lorcan.

'Am I glad to see you,' she said, rushing up to clasp his arm and rest her forehead against his shoulder.

After her fear, she needed to touch him. She needed his strength. She needed some comfort.

He grinned. 'It's that bad, eh? Ditto. My loins are aching for you, too.' He drew her closer. 'But with Harriet gone we can—'

Jess stood back. 'You don't understand. It's mission accomplished,' she said proudly.

'Excuse me?'

'I have the kidnappers locked up in the kitchen, though there's a chance they could escape and—'

'The kidnappers?'

'There're two. They were hiding in the garden, but I opened the back door on purpose and they came inside.'

Lorcan swore. 'They've turned up?'

'Yes, and I locked them in the broom cupboard.'

'We must let them out,' he decreed, shepherding her hurriedly into the kitchen where the shouts had ceased and the pounding had become intermittent.

'At least, I think they're kidnappers,' Jess continued as the idea which had shone with such credibility just a few minutes ago suddenly seemed lacklustre. 'Though if they are why would they wait five weeks before making their first move? Careful,' she warned, for he had removed the chair and was turning the key.

As surprise had been the decisive factor in her capturing the youths, so their surprise at the door being abruptly wrenched open—and by a tall, well-built man—held them still and gawking.

'These are the kidnappers?' Lorcan protested as they blinked at him from the gloom.

'I thought so,' she said, 'but now—'

'You used to work at the hotel site,' he said, frowning at the two captives, 'until you decided that labouring was too rough for you.' He jerked his head. 'Come on out.'

Subdued and docile, they shuffled into the kitchen.

'We weren't going to hurt you,' the Indian boy said, giving Jess a sheepish smile.

'We'd only have kept you for a day or two,' added the Creole youth, in a rollingly accented voice. 'Isn't that the truth, Lif?'

'It is, Sonny.'

'Kept me?' she queried.

'You were going to kidnap her?' Lorcan demanded. The intruders exchanged a look.

'We're not saying another word,' the Indian boy declared.

'Yes, you are. You're going to tell us everything,' Lorcan said, and pointed to chairs at the table. 'Sit.'

Clearly recognising the voice of authority, they obeyed.

As Jess sat down opposite them with Lorcan, she sniffed. A smell had come with the youths out of the cupboard. It was a smell which had intensified in the confined space and clung to their clothes. A distinctive smell which she recognised.

'Cheroot,' she murmured, and Lorcan nodded, his eyes meeting hers. He, too, had caught and identified the aroma.

'You were with Gerard Warwick when he was here recently,' he said to the youths.

They looked at him with such slack-jawed astonishment that she almost laughed. How did he know that? was written all over their faces. What else did he know? Mightn't it be best to confess all?

'At the bar in the village,' agreed Lif.

'Yes, though we first met the guy in August,' Sonny rattled off at the same time.

'It'd help if just one of you told the tale,' Lorcan said.

Sonny dug an elbow. 'Go on, Lif.'

'OK, but are you going to hand us over to the police?' his companion asked worriedly. 'We haven't done anything wrong, apart from entering the house—' he darted a glance at Jess '—so—'

'We'll decide when we've heard what you've got to say,' Lorcan said. 'Start at the beginning.'

Lif cleared his throat. 'Back in August we happened to get talking to Gerard Warwick when he came into the bar. We told him we'd seen him when he'd visited the site and that we'd worked there, but we'd packed it in—'

'Labouring is terrible on the fingernails, y'know,' Sonny inserted. 'And ruins your back.'

'—and were looking for work. He asked if we'd like to make some money. Big money. When we asked how he told us he wanted to have some guy and maybe his daughter taken hostage for a few days and released for a ransom.'

'Our money was going to come from the ransom,' Sonny explained.

Lif might have been acting as narrator, but it was becoming clear that they operated as a double act.

'Gerard asked if we could suggest some place out of the way where the hostages could be held and we mentioned the Rivière Noire—'

'Black River,' Sonny said.

'Thanks for the translation,' Lorcan told him drily.

'—gorges. There are nooks and crannies there, where runaway slaves used to hide in the olden days.'

Jess glanced at Lorcan. 'Gerard didn't say who the hostages would be?'

'No,' Lif replied. 'Though it didn't matter because about a month later he telephoned my house from London and told us to forget the whole idea.'

'So we didn't get a single rupee,' Sonny said, and shrugged. 'Mind you, we hadn't decided whether we'd do it anyway. If the guy we kidnapped had cut up rough we could've got hurt, y'know?'

'I know,' Lorcan said.

'And we didn't want to risk that.'

'Not last weekend, but the weekend before, Gerard Warwick walked into the bar again,' Lif continued, in his precise sing-song voice. 'He sat us in a corner with a drink, blew smoke all over us, gave us a handful of his expensive cheroots and declared that his talk of kidnapping had been a joke.'

'It wasn't,' Sonny said, gazing earnestly out from beneath his fringe of dreadlocks. 'The guy'd meant it.'

'We thought we'd never hear from him again, but yesterday he rang from Cape Town. He wanted to know if we could take you to the Black River for a couple of nights—' the youth shone a nervous smile at Jess '—to collect a ransom and to give you a little scare. Sounded like you'd upset the guy and he wanted to get even.'

'Lif said his voice was slurred as if he could've been drinking,' the Creole youth added.

'So when you came into the kitchen you were planning on kidnapping Jess?' Lorcan demanded.

The Indian boy hurriedly shook his head. 'No, sir. We hadn't agreed whether we'd go ahead and Gerard Warwick wanted it timed at the weekend, when he'd be here and could send a ransom note.' He shifted in his chair. 'But the door was open so we thought we'd take a quick look at the layout of the house. Just in case. If we'd done it, we wouldn't have harmed her,' he assured him fervently.

'If you'd laid one finger on her, you would've had to deal with *me*,' he growled.

Lif gave a fearful smile. 'Yes, sir.'

'Though I doubt you'd have managed to kidnap me in the first place,' Jess observed.

'Wouldn't have been easy,' Sonny agreed, with a wary look at the broom cupboard.

'But we didn't and we realise how wrong it would've been,' Lif said, reaching the end of his recital. He, too, glanced towards the cupboard. Being bundled inside had obviously been traumatic. 'We've learned our lesson.'

Leaning close, Lorcan spoke into her ear. 'Their addresses'll be on the payroll, which means that if we need to locate them again we can. So I suggest we let them go.'

'I agree,' she murmured.

'You're free to leave,' he told the two youths.

'You won't be calling in the police?' Lif asked.

Lorcan looked at her. 'No,' he said, when she shook her head.

'Thank you,' Sonny said, shining a face-splitting smile of relief.

'Yes, thank you so much, both of you. We haven't been in any trouble before and we're going to keep well away from Gerard Warwick from now on,' Lif declared, gabbling out the words in his gratitude.

'A wise decision,' Lorcan said.

'If you're looking for work, you could try the Golden Dragon restaurant,' Jess told the two youths. 'Mr Yap, the owner, needs help in the kitchen.'

'Thanks,' they said, in unison.

Lorcan rose to his feet. 'And now, instead of sneaking in, you can leave the proper way. By the front door,' he said, and ushered them out into the hall.

'What an inept pair,' she said, when he returned.

'But not so inept that they couldn't have taken a swing at you if they'd tried. You opened the back door to draw them inside—what on earth were you thinking of?' he demanded, standing over her with his hands spread angrily on his hips and his blue eyes blazing. 'You may be a spitfire and trained in martial arts, but you were also alone in the house and it was two against one. Something could've gone wrong and—'

'Nothing went wrong,' Jess protested, bewildered to find herself being so furiously chastised. 'Lif is as skinny as an ironing board and Sonny—'

'Has the muscles of Mike Tyson,' he rapped.

'But is no fighter.'

'Which you didn't know when he came inside. As you didn't know whether or not they were carrying knives or even a gun. Did you?'

'Well . . . no.'

'Don't you ever take a risk like that again,' Lorcan stormed. 'Understand?'

She nodded. In her desire to impress him with her prowess, she had, she acknowledged, got carried away and been far too impulsive. 'I understand.'

He glowered at her in silence then, deciding that his message had been properly digested, leant a hip against the table and folded his arms. 'As well as Lif and Sonny being inept, Gerard is pretty half-baked when it comes to kidnap, too,' he said, his tone calmer. 'First he concocts that note in London, presumably to set the scene for the ransom demand which would follow—'

'But also to rattle you, and perhaps in the hope that you'd be scared away from Mauritius and he could grab himself a piece of the action?' Jess suggested.

'Possible,' he agreed.

'And Gerard would know about Charles Sohan calling Harriet your "precious brunette"?'

He nodded. 'We all attend the same business functions from time to time, so he must've heard him and decided to include it as a clever touch. If Harriet and/ or I had been kidnapped, Sir Peter would've come up with the ransom, which would've been useful in settling any gambling debts,' he went on.

'True, but Gerard backed off.'

'Maybe you asking if they'd called in the police made him realise he could be getting in too deep.'

'Or maybe he had a win at the casino which wiped out any debts.'

He gave a dry smile. 'Who knows? But I should've realised he might've sent the note. Hell, all the signs were there.' Lorcan scowled. 'But it would never've occurred to me that he might consider having *you* kidnapped.'

'The signs were there, too,' Jess said. 'When I rejected his advances the other day, I set him against me. He said something about an endgame and he must've been wondering how to take revenge. One evening he had too much to drink and came up with the answer.'

'But he didn't think it through. He knows you're a determined lady and even if he was tipsy it should've occurred to him that amateurs like Lif and Sonny wouldn't stand too much of a chance.' A grin bloomed in the corner of his mouth. 'Unless they'd come armed with cockroaches.'

'I notice you retain a sense of humour,' she said. 'I like that.'

The grin curved full-blown across his lips. 'Glad to know I please.' His blue eyes gleamed. 'And in other ways, too.'

'So what do we do now?' Jess asked, refusing to be sidetracked. 'I know that Gerard ought to be reported to the police, but if we report him we're virtually bound to implicate Lif and Sonny.'

'Yes, though all we really have is hearsay so it'd be difficult to prove anything.'

'And if we made an official complaint his father would be disgraced and would suffer.' She frowned. 'I wouldn't want that.'

'Nor me. Suppose we talk to Sir Peter when they stop over at the end of the week, tell him what Gerard's been up to and let him take whatever action he thinks fit?' he suggested.

She nodded. 'Good idea.'

'I also need to talk to you,' Lorcan said gravely, 'about the possible identity of the kidnappers. When you told me you'd caught them—'

'You thought you knew who they were,' Jess broke in. 'You spoke about them turning up and you were surprised when they were Lif and Sonny.'

He nodded. 'I assumed you must've caught my sister-in-law, Fleur, and her husband, Boris.'

She stared at him. 'You bastard, I knew it!' she exclaimed. 'I knew you were hiding something. I knew you were tricking me.'

'Not tricking, Jess,' he protested.

'You deliberately withheld facts. Relevant facts which, as Harriet's minder, I needed to know,' she said, the yellow flecks spitting indignantly in her hazel eyes. 'That is trickery. And it's downright stupid!'

Lorcan frowned. 'Guilty on both charges,' he said.

'How do you expect me to do my job properly if you obstruct me?' she demanded. 'I can't. I have to be fully briefed, otherwise—'

'I didn't keep quiet in order to make things difficult for you,' he cut in. 'I kept quiet because it was easier for me. I made a mistake.'

She glowered. 'And this couple could appear in Mauritius and try to snatch Harriet?'

'There's a chance, though how real it is I don't know. Just before we left England, I received a letter from my sister-in-law stating that she knew I was working here and that I was taking Harriet with me for a while. She accused me of disrupting her life, again, and said, again, that she'd be much better off with her.' The pulse throbbed in his temple. 'I could've been overreacting, but to me the letter read like a threat.'

'Which is why you decided to employ me at the last minute?' she demanded.

'Yes.'

'And your sister-in-law's made similar remarks before?'

'She's been making them for two years.' He raked his fingers through his hair. It seemed a lonely gesture. 'The longer it goes on, the worse it gets. If Harriet's out with someone and they're five minutes late I start to panic, and sometimes I get up in the night and go into her room to check that she's still there.'

Jess looked at him. It was difficult to stay angry when he was so troubled and when she longed to put her arms around him, stroke his back and say 'There, there.'

'I'm sorry,' she said.

Lorcan gave a bleak smile. 'So am I.'

'Your sister-in-law is keen to take charge of Harriet?'

He nodded and, taking a chair from under the table, he straddled it. 'Fleur is ten years older than Sara— they had different mothers—and although she and Boris have been married for around fifteen years they've never had children,' he started to explain. 'They want them desperately, but despite having all kinds of tests and being assured that nothing's wrong Fleur has failed to conceive. When Sara died, she and Boris offered to look after Harriet.'

He rubbed his forehead against the top bar of the chair. 'They didn't just offer. Fleur more or less insisted it was my duty to hand her over. She said, quite truthfully, that they could offer Harriet a steady home with two parents, whereas I was a guy on my own whose work meant I was often on the move.'

'But you weren't inclined to hand her over?'

'No. One way and another, the two of us had been through a lot together—'

'Your wife being killed?'

'That, and—' He broke off. 'Yes, Sara's death was traumatic. When I said I wanted to bring up my child by myself, Fleur accused me of rank selfishness and declared that she and Boris would sue me for custody in the courts.'

'That seems extreme,' she protested.

'My sister-in-law is an extreme and highly strung woman. Her husband is also extremely wealthy, which means they can hire the most cunning and ruthless lawyers. Although I believed I had a strong case for caring for Harriet, there are certain facts from the past—' his face took on a shuttered look '—which could be twisted to their advantage. I didn't relish the thought of being mauled by their paid Rottweilers, so before any legal wheels could start turning I moved out of state. However, Fleur continued to talk of taking me to court and eventually I went back to England, which put me out of her orbit, plus it gave Harriet the added family security of my parents. Sara was the daughter of Tony Rocca,' he continued slowly. 'He's—'

'The film director. I know,' Jess cut in. 'Gerard said.'

Lorcan frowned. 'Well, Fleur also threatened to inform the media of my "cussedness" as she calls it. She reckoned they'd be interested because of the link with her father.' His frown cut deeper. 'I'd hate it if my life became gossip column fodder, but what I'd hate even more, what I'd *detest*—' he spat out the word '—is for Harriet to be hassled.'

'Does she know that her maternal grandfather makes films?'

'No, nor is she aware of his other, more dubious claims to fame,' he said drily, 'and, for now, I'd prefer it to stay that way. I hoped it'd be out of sight, out of mind and Fleur would forget about acquiring Harriet,' he continued, 'but the woman doesn't give up easy. I only discovered it by chance, but when I was in the States she hired private investigators to check on me—'

''Struth!'

'Where I went, when, and what I did.'

'To see how closely involved you were in Harriet's life?'

'And to try and dig up some dirt.' His mouth twisted into the mockery of a smile. 'Fleur would've loved to have been told that I was drinking heavily, or doing drugs, or sleeping around, then she'd have used it as evidence that I was an unsuitable father. But her sleuths were unable to dig up anything.' He looked at her across the back of the chair. 'You're the first woman I've slept with since Sara.'

Jess felt a pang. By saying 'first woman', he made it sound as though she was just one at the head of a line and, whilst flavour of the month right now, destined to be superseded.

'So your sister-in-law hasn't attempted to get custody?' she asked.

'Not so far as I'm aware, though Californian law can be a strange beast and has long arms. But she hasn't stopped trying to persuade me to hand over Harriet of my own accord. When dredging up dirt failed, she bombarded me with phone calls, telling me what a wonderful life she could have with her, how a little girl needed a mother, that a regular routine was essential for a child's well-being.'

'All of which contained sufficient grains of truth to make you feel guilty?'

'You guessed. I don't know whether or not it's my Irish blood, but I seem to be good at guilt, good at brooding, too.'

'You brood beautifully,' Jess told him.

He smiled. 'Thanks. A few months ago, Fleur started to hint at kidnap,' he continued, his expression sobering. 'She said that when I was away on business maybe she and Boris'd appear and take

Harriet back to the States. And that if I kicked up a fuss they'd hide her some place where I'd never find her.' His expression was grim. 'It sounds dramatic and I'm surprised at Boris going along with that kind of idea because he's a nice guy, yet you do read about kids disappearing.'

'Would Harriet know Fleur if she met her?'

'No, she was only two when they last met. But she is aware that she has an aunt Fleur and although I've said she mustn't go off with her if she should put in an appearance it's possible she could be persuaded.'

'She might go if Fleur spoke about her mother.'

Lorcan nodded. 'I ought to have told you about all this at the start, but I couldn't decide whether or not Fleur was shamming or if her threats were genuine. I still can't. But also I don't find it easy to talk about my private life,' he said, his face taking on the shuttered look again, 'so I went the easier route and decided to keep quiet. Forgive me?'

Jess sighed. 'I do.'

'Thanks.' Rising, he swung the chair back under the table. 'Bedtime,' he declared.

She stood up. 'You haven't had your dinner,' she said. 'It's in the fridge. I'll get it.'

As she went to move past him he caught hold of her waist, holding her still. 'I don't want any dinner,' he said softly. Raising a hand, he started to undo the row of pearl buttons which went down from the V neckline of her dress. 'I only want you.'

'But you've been working hard and it's tasty,' she started to protest.

He had opened three buttons, revealing the smooth tanned fullness of her breasts in her low-cut bra. He stroked his fingertips across one curve, into the scented valley between, and across the other. 'You're tasty,' he murmured.

Jess drew in a breath. By making love whenever Lorcan wanted, she was being far too amenable. She must not always agree, agree, agree.

'You need food,' she declared.

Sliding a hand down over the line of her hip, he pulled up her skirt. As she felt his touch on her naked thigh, she closed her eyes. His finger was pushing beneath the white lace of her panties, touching and gently probing. She clenched her teeth. She would not cry out in delight. She would not react. But as his finger probed deeply her body shuddered and a moist warmth flooded between her thighs.

'I need you,' Lorcan said, and knelt.

He eased aside the white lace and as his tongue licked over the glistening wing of her sex she gripped at his shoulders. When he tasted her essence, she whimpered; she could not help it.

He looked up at her, his blue eyes soft. 'Bedtime?'

'Bedtime,' Jess agreed huskily.

This time their lovemaking was different. The feverish haste had gone, replaced by a gentleness, a depth of feeling, a calm intensity. The kisses they shared were slower and when they were naked and Lorcan trailed his fingers over her it seemed as if touching her comforted him. As if he drew strength from her. As if his languid worship of her body was somehow...healing.

He slid into her. 'Jess,' he muttered. 'God Almighty, *Jess.*'

His hips began to move and she felt him deep inside her. She moved with him. This was not giving and taking, she thought dimly, this was sharing. She did not know where she ended and he began. They were together—not just bodily, but emotionally. They were kindred spirits. Soul mates.

Afterwards, Jess cried.

'My darling,' Lorcan said tenderly, and when she blinked and sniffed and tried to recover she saw that his eyes were wet, too.

'It's never been like that before,' she told him.

He held her close. 'Nor for me. I'm staying with you tonight. All night. I want to sleep with you and wake up with you in the morning.'

She hesitated. She wanted him to stay and yet a small voice warned that if he did their relationship could be changed.

'Harriet isn't here,' Lorcan said, 'so she's not going to know.'

Jess rested against him. If he slept in her bed for just the one night, nothing would be changed.

'So sleep,' she said.

He smiled and drew her closer. 'I will,' he said, 'a little later.'

CHAPTER SEVEN

LAZILY lifting an arm, Lorcan squinted at the black-faced watch which was strapped to his wrist. It was early Monday morning and the alarm had just rung, awakening them.

'By my reckoning Sir Peter and Gerard will've landed, arrived home and, by now, the heir apparent should have repacked his case and be travelling up to Birmingham,' he said, and grinned at her across the pillow. 'To begin his rip-roaring new job as a porter.'

'You think Sir Peter will make him start right away, jet lag or no jet lag?'

'I'm sure of it.'

Recalling the older man's mood the previous day, Jess nodded. 'He was furious—and ultra-determined.'

When Lorcan had taken his visitors for another look around the site on Saturday, he had said he needed a private talk with Sir Peter. And as Gerard had scowled, peeved at being excluded but otherwise un-perturbed, a meeting had been arranged for the following afternoon.

The businessman had been surprised when Jess had accompanied Lorcan into the hotel suite, but as he had listened he had understood the reason for her presence. He had also understood that what they told him was the truth.

'My son's activities have been criminal!' he had de-clared, pacing furiously up and down.

'We spoke to Lif, the Indian youth, this morning and Gerard hasn't been in touch,' Lorcan had said,

146

'so he's obviously abandoned the idea of Jess being kidnapped. What appealed when he had a few drinks inside him didn't hold the same attraction once he'd sobered up.'

'But to have had the idea at all borders on terrorism!' Sir Peter had proclaimed. 'Because his mother walked out and he never knew her I've always felt I needed to make it up to the boy, but I've been far too lax. Far too blind to his faults. No longer!' he had announced, slamming a fist into his palm. 'There's still time to knock Gerard into shape and make a decent human being out of him and I shall do my damnedest! If he wants to take over the company and inherit my wealth, he'll have to work for it. And instead of letting him start at the top he must start at the bottom. He can begin with six months as a porter at one of the hotels.'

Jess had visualised the young man's penchant for designer clothes, his plummy voice and know-all swagger.

'A porter?' she had demurred.

Sir Peter had given a brisk nod. 'In Birmingham; that'll get him away from those loudmouth pals of his. Never did like them. And periods as a waiter, barman and desk clerk will follow. And he can enrol in an AA programme. Tough love, I believe they call it, but essential for someone who needs a lesson in humility and how to relate to his fellow men. And excellent training for a boy who expects to become the head of the Warwick Group.' He had looked out of the window at the ocean where a floating mess of red and white sail gave evidence that a windsurfer had ignominiously collapsed. 'The moment Gerard sets foot on dry land, he will apologise to you.'

Lorcan had shaken his head. 'No, thanks.'

'I don't want an apology, either,' Jess had said.

They had agreed that to demand regrets from a sullen and rebellious Gerard would be pointless. Any apology was bound to be given with bad grace and could harden his vindictive streak. It seemed preferable to leave him to personally acknowledge his mistakes and hope that, with time, he might feel inspired to say sorry himself.

Sir Peter had acceded to their wishes, and declared that as soon as his son returned he would be issuing the severest of reprimands and laying his new code of conduct on the line.

'And now, as Gerard psychs himself up for six months of suitcase-carrying,' Jess said, 'it's time for you to go back to your own room.'

Winding a muscled arm around her, Lorcan drew her nearer. 'Not yet.'

'Yes.' She pressed a hand against the tanned wall of his chest. 'Harriet'll soon be waking up and if she realises you're with me it'll distress her.'

Their supposedly single night spent together while the little girl was lodged next door had been followed by another when she had come home, and another and two more. Each time Lorcan had insisted he *needed* to sleep in her bed, each time Jess had protested, but each time she had given in. And each morning he had had to be pushed out.

'We don't know that,' he said.

'I do,' she declared. 'Harriet wouldn't like you being here, would decide it was my fault and regard me as the enemy. I don't want my relationship with her to fall to pieces. I don't want her to—'

'How about stopping talking and—' he slithered her hand down between their bodies '—doing something about that? What do you think?'

As she felt the velvet thrust of his manhood, her heartbeat quickened. Her breasts might be tender from last night's lovemaking and her body sated, yet her response to him was immediate.

Jess laughed to cover the need which had begun to pummel in her blood. 'I think you're sex mad,' she said.

'I think you're right.' He grinned. 'How about it?'

'Lorcan, we can't. We shouldn't,' she protested as he started to kiss her. She tried to avoid his mouth— that sculpted mouth, the mouth which did such wonderfully lewd things to her and which excited such violent responses. 'There isn't time.'

'Jess, we can. We should.' He nuzzled at her neck. 'There is time, because the way I'm feeling this isn't going to take too long. Damn,' he complained as the telephone rang in the hall.

'Quick, go and answer it before Harriet wakes up, decides to answer it herself and sees you coming out of my room.'

'Your priorities are all wrong,' he complained, but he rolled out of bed, drew on a pair of boxer shorts and went out.

As the door closed behind him, Jess marched through into the bathroom. Switching on the shower, she stepped beneath it. She was not going to risk him coming back and persuading her to participate in a few moments of hectic bliss!

She had soaped herself, shampooed her hair and was rinsing herself off, when the shower door was pulled open.

'That was Naseem's mother,' Lorcan told her, and stopped.

As if hypnotised, he was watching her as she rinsed, his eyes following her movements as she bent to sluice bubbles from her legs, then straightened with arms held aloft, raising her face to the spray.

Jess shut her eyes. His gaze had made her conscious of how she must look—skin wet-sleeked, water pouring over her breasts, channelling into the secret crevice between her thighs. She sucked in air. Her nipples were starting to stiffen and an inner heat had begun to grow.

She switched off the water. 'Who said?' she demanded, being crisply businesslike.

'What?' He blinked. 'Oh, Naseem's mother. She said Naseem is feeling a little off colour so she won't be in today.'

'Then I'll make breakfast.'

'I noticed there's ironing left from yesterday; I'll do it this evening.'

Jess lifted aside her dripping fringe. She needed to dry herself, to shield herself from his disturbing gaze, but he was standing in front of the towel rail.

'You'll do the ironing?' she enquired.

'If it doesn't get done today it'll cause a backlog which Naseem could take ages to clear.'

'OK, but I didn't realise you could iron.'

'As a lone father I've been forced to tackle all kinds of things and ironing is one of them. Shame you don't get the chance to sunbathe nude.'

'Sorry?'

Lorcan's eyes fastened first on her breasts, which rose in two creamy globes against the general gold of her body, then travelled down to the pale triangle which spread at her thighs.

'Then you'd be tanned all over, though the white parts are—' he wiggled a brow '—tantalising. I can iron up a storm, though one or two of the dresses which my mother's bought for Harriet have been a challenge,' he continued, folding his arms across his chest.' 'I'm also able to cook a range of admittedly fairly run-of-the-mill dishes, usually with eggs or chicken—'

'Would you please pass me a towel?' Jess requested impatiently. The longer he looked at her, the more aroused she was becoming.

'And make beds and clean windows and I'm Grand Prix standard with a vacuum cleaner. I can buy birthday presents for other little girls and wrap them and decorate a Christmas tree.' He moved his shoulders. 'All in all, I'm pretty domesticated.'

'All in all, you are doing this on purpose!'

'Doing what?' Lorcan asked innocently.

'Making me feel like you're feeling.' She flicked water at him. 'Get your knickers off.'

He laughed, stepping out of his boxer shorts and into the shower. 'I thought you'd never ask.'

Steering her back against the tiled wall, he circled his palms on the rigid nubs of her breasts and as she murmured a moan of desire he entered her. Jess angled an arm around his neck. She closed her eyes. There was only Lorcan. The rasp of his hands, just a shade away from rough. The heat of his body against hers. His hardness. He thrust and she moaned again. Then his thighs were moving against hers, moving with hers. The tempo increased and, with a low groan of ecstasy, Lorcan jammed deeper and their bodies convulsed.

After they had showered together, he knotted a towel around his hips.

'I told you it'd be over in minutes,' he said, with a grin, and disappeared.

Jess was drying her hair when she heard Harriet padding along the hall and into his room. He had returned in time, she thought thankfully.

'If I bring a picture home from play-school today, where are we going to put it?' Harriet enquired as they finished breakfast. She frowned at the notice-board which was plastered with specimens of her work and at the fridge door which also acted as an art gallery. 'There's no more room in here.'

'Suppose we start a display in your bedroom, on the wall behind your bed?' Jess suggested. 'If we use blobs of that white fix adhesive, it won't mark,' she said, glancing at Lorcan who nodded his agreement. 'We can buy adhesive today.'

'I think I have some in my haversack,' the little girl declared, and climbed down from her chair. 'I'll go and look.'

'You've turned this place into a home,' Lorcan remarked, when they were alone. 'It was just a house when we arrived, but those—' he nodded at the drawings '—and Harriet's kite which you've pinned up in the hall and the corals and the flowers and the books make it feel lived in. Make it welcoming.'

She smiled. 'I've never thought that *I* was particularly domesticated, but thanks.'

'Thank *you*,' he said, and, reaching across the table, he put a blunt-fingered hand over hers.

Her smile faltered. He was looking at her with eyes which were so soft and blue that her heart had begun to turn somersaults.

'Time you went to work,' she declared.

Lorcan looked at the clock on the wall and grinned. 'Like now.'

Jess cleared away the breakfast pots, collected her painting gear and shepherded Harriet out of the house. She often took Choo to play-school, but Amy had made dental appointments so this morning they were on their own.

With the little girl chattering about how in the afternoon she would be playing with her friend—her bestest friend—they set off along the lane. Jess bit into her lip. She had told herself that if she slept with Lorcan for one night nothing would be changed, but they had slept together and woken up together for several nights now and everything *had* changed. She was falling in love with him.

She curled her fingers around the strap of her sports bag. Last night she had awoken in the early hours and gazed at him through the darkness. She had looked at the hair which was rumpled across his brow, at the thick spread of his lashes, at the smooth lines of his face. She had thought how defenceless and vulnerable he seemed when he was asleep, and yet how masterful he was when awake, and she had silently adored him.

'Wait for me at the road,' she cautioned automatically as Harriet skipped off ahead.

But to adore Lorcan, to fall in love with him, was a journey to nowhere. Except heartbreak. He had said he was not interested in commitment. She had seen how memories of his wife still had the power to affect him. She knew he had remained faithful to the woman for two long years. She had also heard Gerard's report of his marriage. What further proof did she need?

Jess paced on. Her lover's new contentment and the way he had looked at her this morning said that he was becoming fond of her. Fond was not enough. Fond lacked sparkle, intensity, the superabundance of emotion which she craved. Fond was for the birds! Yet fond could be dangerous; it might persuade her to hope that her feelings would be returned, eventually. It was a futile hope.

She must end their affair before it was too late. Her stomach cramped. If it was not already too late. Should she tell Lorcan that in mixing pleasure with business she was breaking rules, being unprofessional and thus felt compelled to quit the job and leave Mauritius? Though not, of course, until she had arranged a replacement minder for Harriet.

Harriet. Her head jerked up. Engrossed in her thoughts, she had momentarily forgotten about her and now she looked ahead to the small figure in ladybird-patterned T-shirt, short blue dungarees and baseball cap. Jess went cold. The child had reached the road and started to skip blithely across, but, on her left, a minibus carrying holidaymakers was bearing down. The driver held a microphone to his mouth and, as he spoke, kept glancing back at his audience. He did not appear to have noticed Harriet—and she seemed oblivious of the minibus.

Fear launched her forward. Arms and legs working like pistons, Jess ran. As she ran she opened her mouth to shout a warning, but closed it again. If she shouted, the little girl might stop, turn, look round. And she had to reach the safety of the far kerb before the minibus reached *her*. She must.

Willing Harriet to move faster, faster, she sprinted towards the road. She was almost there when the child jumped onto the kerb and, seconds later, the minibus flashed past. There was no other traffic and, propelled by the momentum of her fright, Jess flew across.

'You could've been killed!' she cried, grabbing hold of Harriet by the shoulders. 'I told you to wait and yet you went over on your own. And you didn't do your kerb drill, you naughty, naughty, silly girl!'

Startled by her fury, the child gazed up from beneath the peak of her cap, then her mouth quivered and her big blue eyes filled with tears. 'You're hurting me,' she said.

'If that minibus had hit you, you'd be hurt much worse!'

Harriet sniffed and stuck her thumb in her mouth. 'I hate you,' she declared, taking noisy sucks.

'I hate you, too,' Jess threw back, then wrapped her arms tight around her, holding her close. She had not known she could feel so terrified or so angry— or be so relieved. 'No, I don't. I care about you, which is why I don't want you dead.'

'Somebody misbehaving?' a voice asked jovially.

It was one of the other mothers taking her children to play-school.

'Do you really care about me?' Harriet enquired as Jess got her ready to play that afternoon.

They had had a sandwich lunch and were in Harriet's bedroom. The little girl stood facing her, while she sat on a dressing stool to brush her hair and tie her ribbon.

'Yes, I do,' she replied, 'even though you did give me the fright of my life this morning.'

Harriet pouted. 'The minibus wasn't that close.'

'Perhaps not,' she admitted, thinking that, in retrospect, she might have panicked, 'but it seemed close at the time and I was scared.' She tugged at a dark curl. 'So in future wait at the kerb.'

'Yes, Jess. I will, I promise. Senga never cared about me,' the little girl went on solemnly. 'When I told Grandma she said Senga loved me, but I knew that she didn't.' Two little arms slid up around her neck. 'You love me, don't you?'

Pulling her onto her knee, she hugged her. 'Of course I do.'

Harriet smiled. 'I love you, too.'

'We love each other, which is how it should be,' Jess said, and was struck with a sudden chilling thought of her one-sided love for Lorcan. She neatened the hair ribbon. 'Now it's time for me to take you round to Choo's.'

As usual, Amy pressed her to come in for a coffee. She stayed chatting for half an hour, then took her leave. The Chinese woman always kept a close eye on the two little girls so Harriet would not go astray, and she wanted to do the ironing. It might be a chore, but it would be unfair to expect Lorcan to do it at the end of the day. And after ironing she wanted to finish the water colour which she was painting of the bungalow.

The ironing had been done and put away, and Jess was setting up her easel on the back veranda, when the doorbell rang. She walked in through the house. Could this be Lif and Sonny? Following her suggestion, they had applied for work at the restaurant and Michael Yap had agreed to give them a trial. She had warned Amy not to expect too much, but so far her protégés were proving to be industrious and keen. They had called round twice to thank her again for the idea, give an update on life in the kitchen and to advise that, as Lif said with a wobble of his head, they were 'keeping to the straight and narrow'.

However, the people on the doorstep were a man and woman in their mid-forties. The man had grizzled grey hair and the lumbering build of a bear, while his partner was a pencil-thin brunette with a smooth, sophisticated bob which did not move. Both wore pastel-shade shirts and trousers of the 'smart casual' variety and looked a little worn.

'Is this the Hunter household?' the man asked, in a low growly voice with an American twang.

'It is,' Jess replied.

'We're Mr and Mrs Ulrich. Fleur here is Mr Hunter's sister-in-law,' he explained, indicating his wife, 'and my name is Boris.'

Her grip on the door tightened and her head began to pound. Last week she had rated the chance of kidnap as a thousand to one, but for a second time the odds seemed to have drastically shortened.

'Good afternoon,' she said.

Boris smiled. 'I guess Mr Hunter'll still be at work?'

Jess hesitated. Whilst she did not want to divulge any information which they might find useful, there seemed little point in claiming that Lorcan was here and being unable to produce him.

'He is,' she confirmed.

Fleur heaved a sigh. 'We thought so.'

'We need to speak with him,' her husband explained, 'but we don't have too much time and we'd very much like to speak with him today.'

'Perhaps we could come in and wait?' Fleur suggested, looking beyond her into the hall.

She thought fast. Whilst she was wary of the couple, it seemed doubtful they would appear at the door and announce names and identities if they were hell-bent on abduction. Their manner did not hint at any immediate threat, either. Indeed, Boris, in particular, seemed anxious to be friendly. It could all be a pretence, but the decisive factor in allowing them into the house was that Harriet was not around.

She nodded. 'I'll telephone and ask if Mr Hunter's free to come and speak to you now,' she said as she showed the couple through to the living room. 'It won't take him long to get home.'

'That'd be real kind,' Boris said, sinking down into a chair. 'We're a little wrecked. We have a vacation booked in the Maldives but made a special side-trip down to Mauritius first to see Lorcan, and it feels like we've been travelling for ever.'

'It's two days since we set off from LA,' Fleur added, and turned down her red-lipsticked mouth. She looked around. 'Harriet isn't here?'

'No, she's away playing with a friend for the afternoon,' Jess replied carelessly, trying to give the impression that the friend lived many miles distant and praying that Harriet would not suddenly take it into her head to come back for some reason. 'I'll ring Lorcan now,' she said, and sped into the hall.

Lifting the telephone, she dialled Amy's number.

'It's Jess,' she said quietly, when her neighbour answered. 'Could you hang onto Harriet and not let her come home for at least another hour, or better still two? I can't explain right now, but it's important.'

'No problem,' Amy replied. 'Suppose she stays with us and has her dinner?'

'That'd be ideal. Thanks,' she whispered, and ended the call.

Next she rang the site office. 'Could I speak to Mr Hunter?' she requested, speaking in a louder voice. 'Tell him it's Jess and it's urgent.'

'You're in luck, he's just walked in,' came the reply. 'Here he is.'

'Something wrong?' Lorcan asked.

'Your sister-in-law and her husband are with me,' she said, and briefly explained.

He muttered an oath. 'They've seen Harriet?'

'No.' Jess spoke softly, her back to the living room. 'She's playing with Choo.'

'Get hold of Amy and tell her to keep her there.'

'Already done.'

'Thanks. Have they given any clues as to why they're here?'

'No. They just said they wanted to speak to you.'

She could feel his tension coming down the line. 'That sounds ominous.'

'So I told them I'd ring to see if you're able to come home.'

'I'm on my way,' he told her, and the line went dead.

Returning to the living room, she advised the visitors that Lorcan would soon be back and asked if they would care for a drink.

'Coffee, tea, beer, lime juice, cola?' she recited.

'Lime juice sounds good,' Fleur decided.

'And for me,' said Boris. 'We overheard you saying your name is Jess,' he remarked, when she returned with a tray carrying a jug and glasses. 'May we ask— Jess what?'

'Jess Pallister.' She hesitated. 'I'm looking after Harriet.'

'Lucky Harriet,' he said, and winked.

Jess smiled. His combination of bulk and affability gave Boris Ulrich an attractive avuncular air. She could not help but like him, though she was not so sure about his wife.

As they made small talk about the hazards of long-haul travel and the charm of the island, she secretly studied her. She would never have guessed that the woman was related to Sara Hunter. Lorcan had said they had had different mothers and it was to Fleur's disadvantage. Where the younger sister had been petite and beautiful, the older one was of medium height, dieted down to X-ray thin and plain. Her face might be carefully painted, her nails manicured an expensive blood-red, her hairstyle chic, but it was impossible to disguise her sharp features and her swarthiness.

Lorcan had referred to his sister-in-law as highly strung, she remembered. And this was evident in the way Fleur perched on the edge of her chair, uttered the occasional startlingly shrill laugh and constantly revolved the wide gold bangles which were looped around her wrist.

Throughout the conversation, Jess had one ear on constant alert for the Jeep, and when she heard the crunch of tyres she leapt up.

'Excuse me,' she said, going out to open the door and find Lorcan already coming up the steps two at a time. 'Everything's OK in that direction,' she told him, with a nod towards the house next door.

Wrapping an arm around her, he held her close against his heart for a moment. As she had needed to take comfort from him when scared that Lif and Sonny might have an accomplice, so in his time of trouble he felt a need to touch her.

He released her, set his broad shoulders and strode into the living room.

'Fleur. Boris,' he said. 'What a surprise.'

The older man started to get up out of his chair to greet him. 'Yes, we—'

Lorcan stopped him short. 'You're here to tell me you've finally acquired some piece of paper which demands that I relinquish Harriet into your safe-keeping?' he said, his voice harsh and his blue eyes ice-cold. 'You've wasted your time and money.'

'But Lorcan—' Fleur began.

'You claim you can give her a good life, but I *am* giving her a good life. This might be a temporary location, but Harriet is happy here. Contented. And she'll be contented in the future because she'll be with me and Jess.'

'Jess is her nanny,' Fleur said, revolving her bangles like crazy. 'We know.'

He shook his head. 'She isn't her nanny. Jess is a bodyguard and an excellent—'

'A bodyguard?' Boris protested. Frowning at his wife, he rose to his feet. 'You believed Harriet was in such danger from us that you needed to employ someone to protect her?'

'After two years of constant demands that I hand over my daughter, after being spied upon, after receiving Fleur's last letter, you're damn right I did,' he scythed.

'Oh, Lord,' the older man muttered, shaking his head.

'But from now on Harriet will have a father *and* a mother because Jess and I are setting up home together.' He placed his arm around her shoulders. 'Yes?'

She swallowed. His statement might only be a smokescreen blown out on the spur of the moment and for the moment, but it still made her nerves tingle.

'Yes,' she replied.

'We've only just decided and no one else knows, not even Harriet,' he continued, 'but she'll be delighted because she thinks the world of Jess.'

She bobbed her head. At least his last phrase contained some degree of truth. 'We get along well.'

'Harriet will have a steady life with us, a settled family existence,' Lorcan rasped. 'So you can get your lawyers to do their worst, but no court will find in your favour now!'

'Calm down,' Boris appealed.

His nostrils flared. 'You ask me to be calm when you *still* have your private eyes checking up on me and reporting back? It was them who provided the information that I was here and Harriet would be with me for a while,' he said, when the older man looked puzzled. 'And who came up with this address.'

'No, I was told of your location by a guy I met who'd worked with you in California,' Boris said. 'He'd heard about it on the construction grapevine, plus the gossip that you were intending to give your daughter a taste of sunshine.'

'And I rang the Warwick Group's London offices, explained that I was related and asked if they could tell me where you were living,' Fleur added.

'The investigators were paid off a long time ago,' Boris went on. 'Just as soon as I discovered that Fleur had employed them.'

Lorcan frowned. 'You didn't know?'

'No. Neither did I know that she'd continued to harass you. But we're here because Fleur wishes to apologise and—'

'Apologise?'

He gave a bitter laugh. A laugh which made Jess wince and which went straight to her heart. His sister-in-law had condemned him to two years of continuous worry, two years of hell, and she wanted to say sorry? Words were not enough. How could anything ever be enough?

'We also want to explain,' Boris said, and indicated a chair. 'If you would sit down and listen. Please,' he appealed when Lorcan did not move.

It went deathly quiet in the room.

Jess waited. It seemed as if he might order the couple to take their apology and explanation and get the hell out of the house, but after a long moment he nodded.

'Although when Sara died I believed, like Fleur did, that Harriet would be better off with us, I soon realised how determined you were to keep her and how much she meant to you,' Boris began, when everyone was seated. 'I respected your wishes and accepted that you had first claim. I also recognised the value of Harriet being brought up by her father.'

Jess looked at Lorcan. He was now outwardly calm and controlled, though she could sense the anger burning inside him.

'So how come the two of you were planning to file a lawsuit and testify against me in an attempt to get custody?' he enquired.

'We weren't. Fleur lied,' the older man said heavily. 'Believe me, there is no way I would've agreed to a scheme like that.'

'My longing for a child had gotten so obsessive that I was prepared to do anything, say anything which seemed to hold out a hope of making it happen,' Fleur told him. 'I was sick.'

'I had no idea she was writing to you, calling and talking about taking Harriet away,' Boris continued. 'It was only when she went into therapy and realised how mixed-up and neurotic she'd been that she confessed.'

'Therapy?' Lorcan asked.

'It'd reached the stage where her obsession with wanting a child was taking over her life and ruining our marriage. It had become all she ever thought about, so I suggested she should see a therapist.' Boris looked at his wife. 'She resisted at first, but it's been so beneficial.'

Fleur uttered one of her shrill, startling laughs. 'Saved my sanity.'

'She started attending the clinic more than a month ago—'

'Just after I wrote to you,' Fleur inserted.

'—and from that very first session her attitude altered. Now she's confronted the reality that chances are we'll never have kids and is rethinking the future and rebuilding her life. And an essential part of the rebuilding depends on her facing you and apologising.'

'I do apologise,' Fleur told Lorcan. 'I ignored your rights as a father and thought only of myself. I didn't even think of Harriet's needs, not in any depth. I've been so selfish,' she declared and, clasping her hands together, she embarked on a long and devout expression of shame.

The self-chastisement had obviously been her therapist's idea, Jess thought drily as she listened, and when Fleur reported back she would be given full marks. Though whether the woman had any inkling of the turmoil she had caused seemed doubtful.

'So if you can find it in your heart to forgive her,' Boris said as the diatribe came to an end, 'we would both be grateful.'

'I'll try,' Lorcan said.

The older man got up and went over to put a hand on his shoulder. 'Thank you.'

'I don't suppose there's a chance of snatching a quick peek at Harriet before we leave?' Fleur asked hopefully.

Lorcan frowned and looked at Jess. She nodded. The apology might have been more for his sister-in-law's benefit than his, but now was a time to bury the hostilities of the past and start again.

'Sure,' he said.

She rose to her feet. 'I'll get her.'

After advising Amy that all was well but there were guests who wished to briefly meet Harriet, she took the little girl home.

'This is your aunt Fleur and uncle Boris,' Lorcan explained as they entered the living room.

Harriet smiled politely, if a little vaguely. She had been playing with Choo on her toy computer and she was keen to get back.

'You're still so cute!' Fleur exclaimed, grasping hold of her hand. 'When you were a tiny girl, your mommy and I used to take you with us when we went out to lunch. You would sit on a cushion on your chair like a princess, and the *maître d'* and the waiters and all the other diners would just *drool* over this gorgeous child. Do you remember?' she asked, peering into her face.

Harriet tried to step away, but couldn't because her hand was so tightly held.

'No,' she said.

Her aunt looked disappointed. 'Do you remember me and Uncle Boris?'

The little girl subjected her to a frowning look and turned to study Boris. 'No.' With a jerk, she freed her hand. 'Can I stay the night at Choo's house?' she asked, her gaze swinging between Lorcan and Jess.

'We haven't asked her mummy yet, but she won't mind and—'

'It's fine by me,' Lorcan said.

'Goody!'

'We must be on our way,' Boris declared, and as he explained how they had seats booked on a flight to the Maldives that evening and a car and driver waiting down the lane everyone went outside.

'If you want to visit and see Harriet any time, let me know,' Lorcan said.

Boris smiled. 'Thanks. And thanks for taking this so well. If I'd been you, I reckon I'd have torn Fleur limb from limb.'

'It was close,' he said tautly.

As the visitors left, pausing to give one last wave before they turned out of the drive, he wrapped an arm around Jess's shoulders.

'My worries are over, thank God,' Lorcan said with feeling, and he kissed her.

She had barely had time to absorb the warm pressure of his mouth when a small foot stamped down hard on the gravel.

'Stop it!' Harriet ordered.

Jess pulled back. She had known the little girl would consider she was intruding, she thought wistfully, and would not like it.

'I don't want my daddy to kiss you,' Harriet declared, glaring up at them both with a look which would have frozen at the famed forty paces.

'It was just the once,' she said soothingly, 'and it doesn't mean he doesn't love you. He does, very much.'

Lorcan went down on his haunches in front of his daughter. 'I'll always love you, fishface.'

A small hand pushed at his chest. 'But Jess is mine and you're not to kiss her! You mustn't have a cuddle. She should cuddle *me*.'

Jess gave a surprised laugh. Harriet was jealous, but in a different way from how she had imagined.

'We could all have a cuddle,' she said.

Lorcan picked up the little girl. 'Good idea,' he said, and as he straightened Jess put her arm around them both.

She kissed Harriet and so did he.

'How's that?' she asked.

Harriet pouted, then grinned. 'Nice.'

'Suppose we ring and ask if you can stay the night with Choo?' Lorcan suggested.

She wriggled out of their arms. 'Do it now.'

Amy was willing and Harriet's night things were quickly assembled.

'I'll take her round and give thanks,' Lorcan said as the child skipped out to the front door. 'Then I'll drive into the village and buy some champagne.'

Jess grinned. 'To celebrate getting Fleur off your back?'

'And to celebrate us.'

'Us?'

'Our new relationship.'

All of a sudden, she was wary. 'Which is?' she enquired.

'When we leave here you'll move in with me,' he said, his expression serious. *'Ciao.'*

CHAPTER EIGHT

THE area of paper above the bungalow was wetted with clean water, then the blue sky colour dropped in at the roof edge and the paint dragged up. Sitting back, Jess assessed the picture. The shade needed to be weakened as it reached the top. Her focus blurred. Her concentration went. At any moment, Lorcan would be returning from the village and she had still not decided what she was going to say to him. How she would cut loose.

She had thought his talk of them living together had been raised as a smokescreen and maybe that was the initial purpose, but now he had decided it appealed to him. And why shouldn't it? she thought wretchedly. He would be co-habiting with a woman who could provide a snug domestic environment, exciting on-tap sex and of whom he was fond. Fond—the word made her want to weep.

Jess sloshed the brush around in the jar of water. Her head was a tangle of thoughts, all of which balled together to form one great big screaming *no*. She could not live with him, knowing she was second best now and for always. Lorcan's gravity had indicated that this was a long-term deal so he was offering a kind of commitment, yet for her it would be a slow death, bleeding away her pride and sense of self-esteem.

Don't fret, one day your prince will come, she told herself whimsically. And he will come free of emotional baggage and unbreakable ties. He will love only you. She filled her brush. But would he be as interesting and funny as Lorcan? Would he add the same joy to her life? Would he—?

She hissed out an impatient breath. Stop it. Where Lorcan was concerned, she seemed to be so vulnerable and pliable and lacking in common sense. Which was why she needed to rehearse a cool, lucid and determined speech which ended their affair.

At the sound of footsteps in the kitchen, her insides clenched. He was back and she did not have one coherent word organised.

'I got two,' Lorcan said, walking out onto the veranda with a bottle of champagne in each hand. He grinned. 'One to say good riddance to Fleur and the other to toast our—'

'I'm leaving.'

'What?'

'As soon as I can get a ticket on a flight I'm leaving Mauritius. Harriet isn't in danger any longer, so there's no reason for me to stay. And even though my contract is for three months I can't allow Sir Peter to pay for me to sit in the sun and paint for the next six weeks. It wouldn't be ethical.'

'I'll explain the situation to him and insist that I settle the account,' he told her.

'No,' she said, feverishly shaking her head. 'It's not the money. It's—well, I think it'd be better to end our relationship now because I don't want to live with you in the future.'

Lorcan strode back inside the kitchen, put the bottles into the fridge and came straight out again. 'Jess—' he began.

'I *can't* do it! I know you'll think I'm being foolish because we're so good together in all kinds of ways and Harriet likes us being together and I like it, too. Much of the time. Most of the time. And if I didn't feel as I do it could probably work. It would work. If I was someone else.'

Jess recognised that any hope of coolness had gone and she was not sure about lucidity, either. 'But I'm determined to try and be a success as a painter,' she carried on, 'and, in any case, I know you'll always love your wife. I know you still do. But I won't be second string, second choice, and there's no way I can fight against a dead woman,' she said, and stopped.

Lifting her brush, she started to hurriedly lighten the sky. She had told herself she would not mention love in any context, because if she did she would be revealing her emotions and exposing her frailty; but the word had sneaked out.

'I don't still love Sara,' he said quietly. 'I never did love her.'

She shot him an impatient look over her easel. 'Lorcan, I've seen the effect her memory has on you. How wound up you become.'

'I become wound up because Sara deceived me, used me and it still hurts. Though what hurt most and what I don't think I'll ever forgive was her attitude toward Harriet.' A painful expression crossed his features. 'She couldn't have cared less about her.'

'She didn't care? Didn't care about her own child?' she said, in bewilderment.

'Not one jot,' he bit out.

'That's terrible,' Jess said, and frowned, recalling the little girl's pride when she had shown off the photographs of her mother. Photographs which she treasured. 'But you've made sure Harriet cares about her.'

He nodded. 'Maybe I'll tell her truth when she's older, but for now I believe it's important that she feels good about her mother and believes that she loved her. Which is why I've always pretended both with her and with others that we were happy together and had a proper marriage.' He gave a bark of mirthless laughter. 'Our marriage was a fiasco!'

She put down her brush. 'Do you want to talk about it?'

'Please. I've kept everything bottled up inside me for so damn long, but it would be a big help if—' he raised his brows '—you're willing to act as therapist.'

'I am.'

Lorcan leant against the balustrade of the veranda. 'I guess I'd better start at day one,' he said, and fell silent for a moment, arranging his thoughts. 'I met Sara when I left Dowling's and landed a job constructing a private house in Los Angeles. The guy who'd commissioned it was big in the production side of the film industry and we became friendly. He was single, several years older than me, but a bit of a swinger. He liked to rub shoulders with movie stars and he took me along to some Hollywood parties.'

'Wow.'

He smiled wryly. 'I've never been particularly starstruck, but I have to admit it was interesting to meet characters whom I'd only ever seen on the big screen. And disappointing. In real life, some of the top box-office actors are so *ordinary*. Sara was at one of the parties.'

'She wasn't ordinary,' Jess observed.

'In no manner,' he said, his voice curt. 'When she got us introduced I felt sure she must be an actress, but it turned out she was an interior decorator and one of Tony Rocca's offspring.'

'She got you introduced?'

'Sara spotted me, liked the look of me and cut a direct path from the far side of the room. Talk about being in the wrong place at the wrong time!' he said blisteringly. 'And once we'd been introduced she made a big play for me. As you know, she was a great-looking girl and I was flattered. Over the next few weeks we met at other parties—I discovered later that she'd engineered it—then she invited me to join a house party at a place which her father owned in Nevada. I accepted. I'd never been to Nevada.'

'But you also liked her?'

'Sure. She was vivacious and friendly, and she had a fund of inside Hollywood stories which amused me. Sara also spoke about her own life—' he frowned '—which was not so amusing. She told me how her father had quit the scene when she was five and that ever since he'd fluctuated between smothering her with generosity one moment and ignoring her the next. And how her mother, who still hankered after him, worked like a demon trying to stay young in order to attract a string of toy boys. Sara's account was blasé, but it was obvious that neither of her parents cared diddly squat about her.'

'Poor girl,' she said sympathetically.

Lorcan nodded. 'It was the flip side of the Californian dream and I felt sorry for her. She'd reckoned there'd be a dozen guests in Nevada, but when we arrived we were alone,' he continued. 'And she proceeded to haul me into bed.'

'You were unwilling?'

'I was . . . doubtful. She'd made all the running and it seemed like she'd got me out there under false pretences. But I was unattached—when I'd left New York three months earlier I'd ended a relationship with a girl—'

'A serious one?'

He shook his head. 'We had fun, but we were both career-minded and not interested in anything deep. Sara was a beautiful girl and I was feeling horny. OK, I was thinking with a part of my body which is not my head,' he said sardonically, 'but we had sex that day and over the next two or three days. I suggested I should take care of protection, but she assured me she'd already done it. When no other guests had appeared by the middle of the week, I made an excuse about needing to get back to work so we returned to LA and went our separate ways.'

'She didn't suggest a further rendezvous?'

'No, though I'm sure she knew that if she had I would've refused. It hadn't taken me long to realise that Sara was unreliable and shallow, and that the only person who counted with her was herself. And you don't need to be Freud to work out that this was because she was riddled with insecurities, due to her childhood being savaged by her father's philandering.'

Jess frowned. 'From what I've read Tony Rocca seems to have moved from one wife to the next, leaving a trail of fatherless children behind him.'

'As well as wives, there've been umpteen mistresses and one-night stands. The guy's life is so fragmented and he has so many kids scattered around that Sara once told me she'd met a boy at a disco, decided she liked him and then discovered he was a half-brother.'

She made a face. 'Creepy.'

'It was six months later before I met her again,' he continued. 'I'd completed the first house and was into another, but I'd remained friends with the producer and had arranged to have lunch with him at a Beverly Hills restaurant. As I was parking my car I saw Sara coming along the street, obviously pregnant. We said hello and I congratulated her—at which point she declared that I should be congratulated, too, because I was the father.'

'Oh, gee. I bet that killed your appetite?'

'Couldn't eat a thing.'

'And you believed her?'

'Yes. The timing seemed to fit and whilst in general I felt she couldn't be trusted on this occasion gut instinct insisted she was telling the truth. And you only need to look at Harriet to know that she's mine.'

'Dimples and all.'

Lorcan smiled. 'Yep. Sara went on to say that her decision to have a baby had gone so swimmingly.'

A line cut between her brows. 'She'd decided?'

'It threw me, too. When I asked her what she meant she informed me that the pregnancy had been planned to the last detail. First she'd selected the type of man she required as the father—tall, dark, healthy and intelligent—then she'd chosen me as an appropriate gene pool. Someone'd told her I was an up-and-coming architect, so my IQ passed muster,' he said drily. 'She'd worked out when she was supposed to be the most fertile, invited me to Nevada and—bingo!'

'She admitted all this to you without any shame?' Jess enquired.

'None. She even thanked me for having a high sperm count and not disappointing her!' His mouth thinned. 'I was furious. Both with her for being so totally manipulative and with myself for being such a sucker.'

'This is why you weren't prepared to take my word about birth control that first time?'

He gave a curt nod. 'I'm sorry. However, when I began to state my objections Sara said I mustn't concern myself because she'd be raising the child on her own and then she walked away.'

'Crikey.'

'My sentiments exactly.' Stretching out an arm, Lorcan reached for a rattan chair and sat down. The sun was setting and he frowned up at the apricot sky. 'After passing through various stages of panic, shock and horror, I knew I *was* concerned. Deeply. Amongst my concerns was how Sara would handle motherhood. The next day I drove to her apartment, but when I raised the subject she declared that the baby had nothing to do with me. I told her to think about what she was saying and pointed out, somewhat emphatically, that fathers have rights, too.'

'It hadn't occurred to her that you might appreciate knowing you'd sired a child and could be interested in playing a part in its life?'

'Apparently not. Nor that the child might appreciate knowing its father.'

'Unreal,' Jess muttered.

'The woman lived in a state of non-reality. Next I asked about finance.'

'Did she make much from her interior decorating?' she enquired.

He shook his head. 'She'd never been trained and although her father had set her up with a shop a few years earlier the business hadn't prospered. Not surprisingly, because Sara had a short attention span and after the first great enthusiasm she seems to have only played at it. By the time we met the shop'd been sold and she was working from home offering what she termed "a professional service", which consisted of giving occasional advice on decor to friends. All it brought in was spending money and Sara liked to spend.'

'She didn't have any savings?'

'She was virtually broke. She admitted she hadn't thought about how she'd pay the bills when the baby arrived, so I offered to make a monthly contribution towards its upkeep.'

'Which she accepted?'

'Without hesitation. I have a strong belief in family values,' Lorcan continued, 'and over the next few days I thought about how I needed to be sure the baby was well cared for and that I'd prefer it to be legitimate. Being a bastard might not be such a stigma these days, but I wouldn't like it.'

'Nor me.'

'I don't even like people knowing Harriet was conceived out of wedlock and I've bent the truth.' He gazed down the length of his long legs. 'The only solution seemed to be for us to be married so after much agonising I suggested it.'

'Did Sara resist?'

'No, as with the money she accepted straight away. I think she'd begun to realise that bringing up a child on her own wasn't such a great scheme, after all. I didn't reckon a marriage of convenience was such a great scheme, either,' he said brusquely, 'but most men would've done the same.'

'Most men would not,' Jess retorted. 'Most men would've told her that as she'd created the situation without either their knowledge or consent it was up to her to cope alone.'

Lorcan moved his shoulders. 'Maybe. Anyhow, a week or so later, we went through one of those soulless marriage ceremonies with no guests and a couple of strangers for witnesses, and she moved into my apartment.'

'And your mother was hurt at not being invited to your wedding.'

'Broken-hearted,' he said. 'My father wasn't too pleased with me, either, though I've since explained the whys and wherefores and now all is forgiven.'

'How was married life?'

'Until Harriet was born we got along OK, though that was because Sara spent most of her time with an actress friend who'd decided that a baby was the ultimate accessory and gotten herself pregnant, too.'

'The actress didn't have a man around?'

'Nope. But once Harriet put in an appearance things went downhill fast.' Lorcan rubbed at his temple. 'I'd always imagined it was human nature for mothers to love their babies, but it didn't happen with Sara. Although she made a fuss of Harriet when other people were around, the rest of the time she was indifferent. She never spoke goo-goo talk to her or tickled her tummy or did all the kinds of things which people do with babies.' He looked at her. 'The kind of things which *you* would've done.'

Suddenly hit with a vision of having his child, Jess managed a strained smile. 'I guess,' she mumbled.

'At first I decided Sara must be suffering from postnatal blues, but after a few months I had to face the fact that she was simply a lousy mother. A non-mother. She had absolutely no feeling for this lovely baby who kicked her fat legs and gurgled.'

'But she'd been pleased to be pregnant, so it doesn't make sense.'

'This is only my theory—reached after endless days, weeks and months of torturous thinking—but I believe because Sara was only interested in herself so long as the baby was a part of her it appealed. Then, when it became a separate person, it didn't. Or maybe

it was a case of after you get what you want you don't
want it.'

'What's your theory on why she wanted a baby in
the first place?'

'I have several,' Lorcan said. 'One, it was a plea
for attention. Two, she was scoring points against
Fleur. They'd always been in competition and dem-
onstrating that she was fertile while her sister remained barren was a big satisfaction. Three, by having
a child without a man in her life—as she'd originally
intended—she was taking some kind of revenge on
her father. Four, she was influenced by her actress
friend—who by then had dumped her baby with a
nanny and gone off on location for a couple of
months.'

'Or it could've been a mixture of them all,'
Jess said.

'True. But once born Harriet became an en-
cumbrance. Sara demanded that I hire a full-time
nurse and started disappearing for long periods on
her own. I was desperate that the baby should feel
cherished, so every morning I'd feed her, change her,
play with her. And the same when I rushed back from
work in the evening.

'Your life must've been hectic.'

'It was, but—' he smiled '—it was all worthwhile
because Harriet was a happy baby.'

'Where did Sara go when she disappeared?'
she asked.

His smile faded. 'Heaven knows, though I'm damn
sure she shed her wedding ring and behaved like a
single girl. She thrived on male attention and when
she crashed her car there was a young lifeguard in the
passenger seat. He escaped without injury.'

'But your marriage was wounding you.'

Lorcan nodded. 'It'd never occurred to me that divorce would be a feature of my life, but if I'd been able I would've been out of there. Fast. Like supersonic. However, I had Harriet to consider. Sara was a casualty of divorce and I didn't relish the pattern being repeated. But my main worry was that if we did separate Sara would decide she wanted the baby to stay with her. And courts tend to find in favour of mothers.'

'You think she might've done that?'

'Again it wouldn't have made any sense, but yes. She could've easily decided she was being deprived, clung on and five minutes later would've been ignoring Harriet again. So I trod water, praying that as the baby grew into a toddler she might suddenly take an interest. I also tried to remember that Sara'd been emotionally damaged and make allowances. I hoped that if she saw me being loving towards Harriet she might realise it was the way to behave and be loving, too.' He gave a harsh laugh. 'It was cloud-cuckooland. She remained indifferent.'

'What was her attitude towards you?' Jess asked.

'Indifference again. We were virtual strangers. We'd slept together a few times when Harriet was small, on occasions when I'd felt compelled to work at the marriage and give it a chance,' he said sardonically, 'but my interest in her had been minimal and she wasn't interested in sex. Although she loved it when guys raved over her looks, Sara was essentially an ice princess.'

'Thanks to daddy.'

'Could be. We didn't connect in any other way, either. When I came back from work you want to know how things have gone, but she never asked a single question. She knew damn all about me and didn't want to know. It seemed like the only question

she did ask was could I give her some more cash—
for clothes, cosmetics, meals out. She soaked me for
every last dollar she could—not like you, who refused
to let me pay for a swimming costume.' His gaze
moved over her. 'You'd look good in it, too. Suppose
we go back to the shop tomorrow?'

She shook her head. 'No, thanks. You were such a
good meal ticket that Sara wasn't inclined to divorce
you?' she asked, guiding him back to his story.

'It seemed so. She seemed content with the status
quo. Plus we slept in separate beds in separate rooms
and I left her alone. I was going insane wondering
what to do, when she took a bend too fast and was
killed.' Lorcan rubbed at his jaw. 'I felt so relieved.
Relieved that she'd died. Can you believe that?'

'Yes, I can,' Jess told him. 'And I think it's entirely
understandable, so don't beat yourself up about it.'

He gave a brief smile. 'No, ma'am. My experience
with Sara left me so bitter and cynical that I swore
I'd never let another woman into my life again. Not
in any meaningful way. I have a healthy
sex drive—'

'Very healthy,' she could not resist inserting.

'—but it lay dormant for ages and then when I did
start to feel the occasional flicker of lust I quelled it
pretty damn quick. It's only since I've known you
that I've felt able to trust a woman again.' His blue
eyes were intent. 'You're honest and kind and prin-
cipled and you've given me back my faith in
human nature.'

Pushing back her chair, Jess rose and went to look
out from the veranda. The apricot sky had darkened
into a glowing umber which was streaked with wisps
of mauve and violet cloud. She turned to frown at
him. Whilst it was good to know she had helped in

his recovery process, she did not want his gratitude. Nor his compliments. She did not want him to be *fond*.

'And as soon as Sara died Fleur proceeded to put you through the wringer,' she said.

Lorcan nodded. 'Earlier I mentioned facts which Fleur could've used against me. When she threatened a lawsuit, she referred to how I hadn't known about Sara's pregnancy and the fact that I hadn't wanted a child. This was true and I could see how lawyers might talk it up and twist it around as evidence that I wasn't a dedicated father.'

'You're a great father.'

He flashed a grin. 'I try. I try. But whereas Sara and I were poles apart,' he went on, 'you and I are on the same wavelength.'

'The first time we met you thought I was a pain in the neck,' Jess protested.

'You thought I was a pain in the neck, too—which proves my point. But I was also attracted to you.'

'Liar, liar, your pants are on fire—as your daughter would say.'

'I'm telling you the truth,' Lorcan insisted, 'and being attracted annoyed me like hell. That's why, even though I wanted Harriet to be guarded, I wasn't too keen on you coming out to Mauritius with me.'

'Not keen? You were downright hostile!'

'OK, but you had trouble written all over you and I've explained how I didn't want trouble. Which, while we're on the subject, seems to be why I employed nannies who had serious boyfriends.'

'You were scared they might fancy you?'

'I didn't consciously think that, but yes. Plus I guess I could also have been scared that I might fancy them. So the nannies were not beauties, like Naseem isn't a

beauty.' Getting to his feet, he went to stand in front
of her. 'But you are beautiful and I fancy you something rotten,' he said, clasping his hands around her
waist. 'When we're married there'll be plenty of time
for you to paint. I promise.'

'Married?' she queried, and heard herself squeak.

'Maybe I'm old-fashioned, but living in sin doesn't
appeal. All right, I said I was happy to have an affair,
and although it took me a month to get around to it
for a while I was. But not now. Now I want us to be
man and wife. I want you and me and Harriet to—'

Snatching hold of his hands, she thrust them from
her. 'But I don't!' she declared, and spinning on her
heel, she strode into the house.

Jess marched through the kitchen, along the hall
and out of the front door. She did not know where
she was going, only that she had to get away. Away
from the man who had sliced through her heart. Away
from the man who could only bring her more hurt.
Half walking, half running, she set off down the lane.

Harriet, she thought. *She* was the reason why
Lorcan wanted them to be married. It was the little
girl's need for a mother which had inspired his pro-
posal. She gulped down a sob. She might not be
second string to his dead wife, but she came second
to his much alive daughter. Fantastic!

She stomped blindly across the road and through
the trees. Reaching the shore, she dropped down onto
the soft sand and glowered out at the lagoon which
shone like charcoal-grey silk in the fast gathering
tropical night. Lorcan had not loved Sara, but he did
not love her, either. Love mattered. For her, love was
all. It might be a romantic notion of the West, but it
was what she believed in. She was damned if she would
enter into a marriage of convenience!

She shot a glance back over her shoulder. She had thought that Lorcan might rush out after her, but she was alone. He must have decided that remaining at the bungalow where he could be contacted should Harriet need him took precedence over following her. It figured, she thought bitterly.

Drawing up her knees, Jess wrapped her arms around them and rested her head. She took a shuddering breath. She had never cried over a man before, but she wanted to cry now. She wanted to weep for her unrequited love and for the partnership which could have been so wonderful—if. Her lips stretched into a bloodless smile. There was no point in ifs, no use in crying.

She listened to the soft suck of the water. Was it too late to pack her cases, take a taxi to the airport and fly out this evening? she wondered. Why not? She could—

'Hi,' a deep voice said, and when she raised her head she saw that Lorcan was standing beside her.

She looked coldly up at him. 'You decided I was worth chasing after all?'

'I thought you were in your room. For the past five minutes I've been standing in the hall appealing to you to come out so that we could talk, then when I finally lost patience and decided to break down the door I discovered it was unlocked, the room was empty and you'd gone.'

'And now you're here to ask me to come back and talk about marrying you?' Jess leapt to her feet. 'Don't waste your breath. I'm still leaving; the only difference is that I'm leaving tonight!' she declared, and sped rapidly away up the beach and into the trees.

'You can't leave,' Lorcan protested, behind her.

'Yes, I can. Maybe it's expecting too much for a London plane to be ready and waiting for take-off, but I know there's a flight to the Maldives so—'

'It'll have left by now.'

'Then I shall pack tonight and leave first thing in the morning,' she declared, her pace quickening as she marched stiffly ahead of him across the road.

'Y'know, when you walk like that your backside jiggles in a way which I find amazingly stimulating,' he said as she raced along. 'What say we head back to the beach, peel off all our clothes and—?'

'Too public,' Jess snapped.

'There's no one around. Besides, where's your sense of adventure?'

'Too gritty.'

'Now that's a point. Get a scattering of sand in the wrong place and it could be painful. OK, we'll wait until we get back to the house—'

She stopped dead. 'I am not going to bed with you ever again!' she declared, spinning around to glare at him, then she swivelled and powered on. 'I can understand that you don't want Harriet to turn out like Gerard, but—'

Lorcan lengthened his stride, which brought him up alongside her. 'Excuse me?'

'You're scared you might fall into Sir Peter's trap of overcompensating and rear a monster. But she won't. Turn out like him.' She swallowed in a breath. Her haste might have brought her back to the house with the speed of an express train, but it was also making her pant. 'You have too much sense to spoil her. Though, in any case, even at four she has far more strength of character.' Striding back into the hall, she gulped in another dose of air. 'So, whilst I don't deny that she'd benefit from a woman's influence while she's growing up, it isn't essential.',

He followed her as she went out through the kitchen and onto the back veranda again. 'You think my reason for wanting to marry you is to acquire a surrogate mother for Harriet?' he enquired.

Jess whipped the picture from her easel and sat it on a chair. Before she started packing her cases, she would assemble her painting gear.

'You bet I do!'

'It's not like that. Not like that at all,' he said, and took a step towards her.

'Don't touch me!' she shrieked.

'The warrior queen strikes again,' Lorcan murmured. 'No one can accuse you of moderation.'

'What?' she asked, but when she looked down she saw that she had grabbed up the jar of water and was poised to fling it at him. 'From champagne to painty water?' she said, putting down the jar. 'That's going too down-market.'

'And you don't usually go around drenching people. Only me.'

Jess bit into her lip. 'Only you,' she said.

'You're wrong about Harriet coming into the equation,' he told her.

She straightened. Her moment of high emotion had gone. Now she was determined to be sensible and matter-of-fact. 'When you talked about us, you talked about her. Perhaps it was subconscious, but that's all the more reason—'

'It wasn't subconscious,' he cut in. 'I was using Harriet to lure you.'

'Lure me?' she said warily.

'I know you care about her and, whilst you must feel something for me because otherwise you wouldn't

sleep with me, I recognise that it's early days yet in
our relationship.' He took a step towards her. 'But I
want to marry you, Jess. And if I don't tell you and
get you to agree somehow, then some other guy might
snap you up. I daren't take the risk. I can't let you
go. And I thought that if I mentioned Harriet— Oh,
damn,' he complained, swiping the swag of lustrous
dark hair back from his brow, 'I'm making a mess
of this. I realise I can't expect you to love me, not
yet, but—'

'How do you know I don't love you?' she enquired.

Lorcan frowned. 'Well—you've never said.'

'You've never said you love me,' she responded.

'Only because I was frightened of rushing things
and scaring you off.'

Jess bit down on a grin. All of a sudden, she wanted
to sing, dance, turn cartwheels.

'It takes a lot to scare me,' she said.

He slid his arms around her waist, drawing her near.
'I love you,' he said huskily. 'And?'

'I love you, too.'

'Darling, my darling Jess,' he said, burying his face
into her hair in a quick gesture of relief. 'So how about
the marriage idea?'

She felt the press of his long body against hers and
listened to the thud of her racing heart. 'I—I think I
could be persuaded.'

'I'd better start with the persuasion now,' Lorcan
said, and, taking hold of the shoestring straps of the
floral sundress which she was wearing, he started to
slide them down from her shoulders.

'I'm not wearing a bra,' Jess protested.

He grinned. 'Goody,' he said, 'to quote you
know who.'

'But we're outside and someone might see us and—' Now she grinned. 'You're right. Where's my sense of adventure? What the hell.'

As his mouth did wonderful things to the column of her throat, he drew the dress down to her waist. When his hands closed over her naked breasts, she closed her eyes and clenched her teeth. His long fingers were stroking, pulling at the tight peaks and sending darts of desire streaking down to her thighs.

One hand moved down over her hip to slide beneath her skirt and caress her backside.

'Beautiful,' Lorcan murmured. 'But now, as we don't want to be accused of outraging people's modesty or whatever they call it out here, I reckon it's time for us to go indoors. And as I'm dirty and sweaty from work—and you're sweaty from that frantic gallop down the lane—I suggest we head for the bath first. And take the champagne with us.'

Jess grinned. 'You are full of the most wonderful ideas,' she told him.

Amidst kisses, a bottle of champagne was taken from the fridge and two wide-necked glasses collected. Amidst kisses, a bath was run. Amidst kisses, they undressed each other.

As she stepped into the warm, scented water, he climbed into the other end of the bath. Swiftly, they soaped and rinsed, then Lorcan uncorked the champagne and filled the glasses.

'Come closer,' he said, and they each slithered to the middle of the bath where they met.

As she put her legs over his legs and sat between his thighs, he handed her a glass of champagne. But before she could take a sip he raised his glass and tipped it over the swell of her breasts.

Jess started. 'Cold!' she exclaimed as the liquid trickled down her. She smiled. 'This is in retaliation for me soaking you in the lift? Seems fair.'

Lowering his head, he licked at a wetted nipple. 'No, it's a fantasy I've had ever since you did.

She drew in an unsteady breath. 'Does it live up to your expectations?' she asked as his tongue caressed the burgeoning pinnacle a second time.

'It's better,' Lorcan said hoarsely, and, taking hold of both their glasses, he placed them on the tiled ledge.

Grasping her hips, he lifted her up and eased her onto him. As she felt the heated thrust of his manhood, she gasped.

'I thought we were having a bath first?' she said.

'So did I.' He smiled a lopsided smile. 'But—'

Now his hands were on her breasts, caressing, fondling, tormenting. Jess tensed. The nerve-ends were bunching between her thighs and as he felt her body tighten around his he held her hips and moved deeper. She trembled, shuddered and cried out.

'My lusty lady,' he said, and held himself still, fighting to control the desire which raged inside him.

When she had quietened, he moved again. And again. She whimpered. To her astonishment, the thrust of him inside her was triggering a second orgasm which gripped even more urgently than the first. And as he felt the tightening and flooding of her body Lorcan allowed himself to follow.

'You're persuaded?' he asked, a little while later.

Winding her arms around his shoulders, Jess smiled. 'Entirely convinced. Yes, I will marry you.'

'When?' he asked, bending his head to suck at the delicate skin of her neck in a way which he knew would mark her as his.

'Tomorrow?'

Lorcan lifted his head. 'I was planning on going to work tomorrow.',

'Excuses, excuses.'

'How about as soon as possible after we get back home?'

'That's another wonderful idea.'

He retrieved and topped up the champagne glasses. 'To us,' he said, smiling.

'To us,' she echoed, and they touched glasses and reached forward to kiss. 'If you're willing I'd like a big old-fashioned family wedding with my parents and my brothers and their families,' she told him as they soaked themselves and idly sipped. 'And, naturally, your parents.'

'I am willing—and they'll love it.'

'Perhaps we should invite Fleur and Boris?'

He hesitated. 'Perhaps.'

'And Harriet can be a bridesmaid.' Her hazel eyes sparkled. 'We could get her to sing her dodo song at the reception.'

'No, we could not!'

She laughed. 'You're the boss.'

'That's a breakthrough,' he said drily. 'But I'm not.'

'No?'

'We're partners,' he told her, his blue eyes serious. 'For now and for ever.'

Jess smiled and leaned forward to kiss him. 'Amen,' she said.

HARLEQUIN ◆ PRESENTS®

Popular author Penny Jordan has worked her magic on
three compelling romances, all complete stories in
themselves. Follow the lives of Claire, Poppy and Star in:

Three women make a pact to stay single,
but one by one they fall, seduced by the
power of love....

Claire is the first to walk down the aisle:
Brad Chandler is sure that beneath her calm exterior
lies a deep passion. Is he prepared to wait for
that passion to reveal itself?
And when it does...

#1883 WOMAN TO WED?

Available in May 1997 wherever
Harlequin books are sold.